Elizabeth Gail

and the
secret love

Hilda Stahl

WindRider BOOKS
Tyndale House Publishers, Inc., Wheaton, Illinois

The Elizabeth Gail Series

Fifth printing, November 1988

Library of Congress Catalog Card Number 83-70037
ISBN 0-8423-0706-0, paper
Copyright © 1983 by Hilda Stahl
Printed in the United States of America

Dedicated with love to the wonderful people at
Thornapple Valley Word of Faith Fellowship

Contents

One
Chance meetings

A tear trickled down her cheek and Elizabeth lifted her hand off the steering wheel to brush it away. "No more crying, Elizabeth Gail Johnson," she muttered as she wiped another one away.

The car swerved a little on the gravel road and Elizabeth quickly clutched the steering wheel with both hands and slowed the small blue Buick. Suddenly it sputtered and jerked and she frowned in dismay. Nothing must happen to Ben's car after he was nice enough to let her take it so she could get away on her own for a while!

The car jerked again and she pulled to the edge of the road, thankful that the ditch was shallow here. What was wrong? Had she ruined Ben's car? She was a responsible eighteen-year-old and not some little kid who wrecked everything she touched!

The hot sun shone through the windows and she quickly opened the door and stepped out onto the rough gravel. Birds sang in the trees that lined the road across from the car. Grasshoppers hopped from the tall weeds near the car and she jumped back to avoid them. Impatiently she tugged her yellow tee shirt down over her dark blue shorts. A pebble lodged in her sandal and she shook it out.

She sighed. What was she going to do now? She was a long way from the Johnson farm and her sandals wouldn't hold up if she tried to walk back to the gas station that she'd passed.

She lifted her pointed chin and squared her slender shoulders. "I won't let this get me down! I won't!" She lifted her eyes to the bright blue summer sky. "Heavenly Father, you always take care of me. Send help to me now when I need it. Thank you."

She looked up and down the quiet road and tried to remember if she'd passed a farmhouse. But she couldn't remember. Her thoughts had been full of her loss. Yesterday she'd gone to Grandma Feuder's funeral. Oh, how could she survive without dear Grandma Feuder?

10

Elizabeth remembered the first time she'd met the short, gray-haired woman who lived just down the road from the Johnson farm. Her great-grandson Adam had lived with her, but the entire neighborhood called her "Grandma." She'd loved it. She was always there to give help and advice and to pray. What great faith she'd had!

Elizabeth smiled softly as she could still hear Grandma say, "Elizabeth, God has given every man a measure of faith. Studying the Bible, then living it, increases your faith."

"Oh, Grandma," whispered Elizabeth as she leaned against the hot car and covered her face with trembling hands. "I didn't want you to leave me."

Chuck had said, "Grandma Feuder is in heaven now. We should be happy for her."

Quickly Elizabeth rubbed away her tears. She *was* glad for Grandma, and she knew someday she'd see Grandma again, but right now it hurt to be without her. Tomorrow Adam would be home again, and he'd be all alone in the farmhouse that he'd shared with Grandma. His sadness would be greater than hers. Somehow she had to help him through this hard time.

She lifted her head, suddenly alert. Dust billowed up and she heard the soft hum of a car. Someone was coming! She smiled. "Thank you, heavenly Father."

Elizabeth got into the car, locked the doors,

11

and rolled up the windows, except for a small crack. It was important to be careful, even so close to home.

She waited, quickly dashing away any sign of tears. She frowned, then grew tense as she recognized the car. Why would Jerry Grosbeck be driving on this road?

She climbed out of the car and wrapped her arms across her reed-thin body as she watched Jerry slide from his old black Pontiac. The long white scar stood out on his tanned face. He stopped and looked down at her with his hands on his lean hips, his feet apart. He was dressed in faded jeans and a striped tank top. "What happened, Elizabeth?" he asked softly.

His dark eyes locked with hers for a few time-suspending seconds. Her tongue felt glued to the roof of her mouth. What was the matter with her? This was the Jerry Grosbeck whom she'd loved as a brother for years. Why was she suddenly feeling so strange? Finally she was able to say, "The car stopped. I don't know what's wrong."

His dark brows pulled together in a frown. "It can't be anything serious. Ben takes very good care of his car."

"I know! I'm just so thankful that you happened along." She frowned. "Just why are you out here?"

He shrugged, then laughed under his breath. It reminded her of all the years when

12

they had lived together as foster kids. She would get angry at him and he'd laugh at her. It was a silent laughter that shook his shoulders and she didn't like it at all.

"Why, Jerry?" she asked sharply, suddenly very suspicious.

He tapped the tip of her nose and she jerked back. "I didn't want you to be alone feeling the way you do."

"Did you follow me?" Her hazel eyes widened.

He nodded. "And it's a good thing I did." He opened the car door and slid under the steering wheel. He turned the ignition key and nothing happened.

"What do you think it is?" she asked in alarm.

"I don't know." He paused, then looked at her and shook his head. "I'll bet you're out of gas, Elizabeth. Out of gas!"

She gasped. "I never thought to check the gauge!"

"It's a good thing I followed you." He stood up, and even though she was tall, he was taller. He leaned down and his breath fanned her cheek. "Aren't you glad I showed up?"

She moistened her lips with the tip of her tongue. "Do you want me to bow at your feet? Kiss your hand? What?"

He chuckled. "None of the above. I just want you to admit that you can't get along

13

without me. I am indispensable to you."

She laughed. "All right, Jerry. Just get me some gas so I can go home."

"Come with me. I'll get gas at the station down the road and bring it back and you can be on your way. Home, I hope."

"I'd better stay here. I don't want anything to happen to Ben's car."

Jerry hesitated, then shrugged. "I won't be long. Do I get my reward now or later?"

"Reward?"

He smiled. "Now *and* later."

Before she knew what he was going to do, he caught her and pulled her close and kissed her. Abruptly he released her and strode to his car and she stared after him, her lips still tingling. Why had he kissed her that way? He wasn't still in love with her. He couldn't be! He'd lost interest almost two years ago.

She watched him maneuver the car until he was headed back the way he'd come. Dust billowed out behind him as he drove away.

She wouldn't think about the kiss. Maybe she'd taken it all wrong. That had to be it. She sighed in relief and turned to open the car door. The sun burned her brown, shoulder-length curls and perspiration dotted her face.

Suddenly a small child's cry rent the air and Elizabeth jerked forward in surprise. She

14

looked around to find the source of the cry, then pushed her way through the tangled weeds until she found a small boy sitting near a bush, his face red, his blond hair damp and tangled.

"Well, who are you?" asked Elizabeth softly as she knelt before him.

He sniffed and knuckled away his tears. "I want to go home."

"I'll bet you do. How did you get here?" Carefully she picked him up and he clung to her as if he was afraid of being alone again. He was about three years old and dressed in tan shorts and a dirty tee shirt. His legs were scratched and his tennis shoes untied.

"I want to go home!"

"I know you do. Where do you live?"

"In a house."

"What is your name?"

"Neddie."

"What is your daddy's name?"

Neddie screwed up his little face. "Daddy."

Elizabeth laughed. "I should have known. I'll take you to my car and then when Jerry comes back, we'll find out where you live and take you home."

"You got any candy?" Neddie rubbed Elizabeth's cheek.

"Sorry, Neddie. I might have some gum in my purse." She stumbled and his grip tightened so much she thought he would choke her. Finally she reached the road again and set him down beside the car. "Jerry will be here soon with gas. The car ran out of gas."

"Where's your gum?" he asked, pulling on the door handle.

A crow cawed and she jumped, then opened the car door and lifted out her small leather purse. She pulled out the pack of gum and handed Neddie one stick.

He ripped off the paper and dropped it to the ground, then stuffed the gum into his mouth and chewed with his mouth wide open.

Elizabeth looked helplessly around, listening for any sounds that someone was looking for Neddie.

With wide gray eyes he looked up at her as if he expected her to find his home without difficulty.

Jerry pulled up and Elizabeth hoisted Neddie to her hip and hurried to Jerry.

"What have you got here?" he asked as he lifted the red can from his trunk.

"I found him," she said, then quickly explained while Neddie chewed the gum noisily, his arm around her and one hand against her throat.

"Can you show us where you live, Neddie?" asked Jerry.

Neddie looked around, then shook his head.

"A little guy like this couldn't walk very far," said Jerry thoughtfully. "I'll put gas in the tank and then we'll drive around a bit to see what we can see."

Elizabeth nodded, then stood and watched Jerry pour gas into the tank. The smell stung her nose and Neddie turned his face against her and pressed his nose into her shoulder.

Several minutes later Elizabeth followed Jerry down the road. Neddie sat beside her, his feet barely hanging over the seat. Dust from Jerry's car blew back to the hood of Ben's car.

Finally Jerry pulled into a drive and Elizabeth stopped behind him. He ran back to her and she rolled the window down.

"I'll go ask here, then wave if you should bring the boy."

She nodded, then watched him run to the old house where a dog barked near the front door. She looked down at Neddie. "Is this your home, Neddie? Is that your dog?"

Neddie scrambled to his feet and stood on the seat and leaned against the dash. "My dog."

"Is it?" she asked hopefully.

"No. I have a green dog." He plopped down and chewed his gum harder.

Elizabeth grinned. A green dog! What did he mean?

Jerry ran back. "The woman here said that there's a farmhouse hidden back off the road

17

near where you found Neddie. I'll lead the way."

Several minutes later Elizabeth followed Jerry down a long drive to a small house that needed paint. A brown dog ran toward the cars, barking loudly.

"Is that your green dog, Neddie?" asked Elizabeth with a little laugh.

"My dog!" shouted Neddie. "My dog!"

Elizabeth stood outside the car and reached in for Neddie just as a young girl ran toward the car, shouting something.

Neddie squirmed and Elizabeth set him down. He ran toward the girl and she grabbed him and shook him.

"We looked all over for you, Neddie!" she cried. "I told you to stay right in the yard! Momma is sure mad!"

Jerry stepped close to Elizabeth and grinned down at her. "The end of a fine adventure."

Elizabeth nodded, then frowned. "I've seen that girl before, Jerry. Look at her closely. Haven't you seen her in church?"

Jerry shrugged. "I don't know."

Elizabeth walked to the girl and waited until she looked up. "Hi, I'm Elizabeth Johnson and this is Jerry Grosbeck. We found Neddie down the road."

"I know you," said the girl, keeping a tight grip on Neddie's arm while the dog licked Neddie's face. "I saw you play the piano in church."

"What's your name?" asked Jerry.

"I'm Diane Vincent. We've only been coming to church for a little while."

"I'd like to see your mother," said Elizabeth.

Diane looked toward the house, then finally said, "She's not feeling very good. But when I tell her you found Neddie, she'll want to see you."

"It pays to be famous," whispered Jerry and Elizabeth smiled.

A brown-haired boy stood just inside the door and Diane said, "This is Shane. We're twins." Then she ran toward a closed door.

"We're both eight," said Shane, eyeing Elizabeth and Jerry.

Elizabeth said hello, then looked quickly around the shabby room. It was messy with toys and clothes lying around.

In a minute Diane walked back with a short, pregnant woman beside her. The woman sank to a chair, then pushed her dark blonde hair back from her puffy face.

"Thanks for bringing Neddie back. We were sure scared but I knew God would send help when we needed it so much."

"This is Elizabeth Johnson," said Diane to her mother. "She plays the piano at our church sometimes."

19

The woman nodded. "I'm Joan Vincent. I do love to hear you play." She looked around and flushed. "I'm sure sorry you have to see the place in such a mess, but I just can't take care of it like I should and David works hard all day in town so he don't feel like doing much in the evening."

"We're just glad we could find you and bring Neddie home safely," said Jerry as he slipped his arm around Elizabeth's waist. "We do have to go now."

"Good-bye," said Elizabeth. She knelt in front of Neddie and hugged him. "Good-bye."

Reluctantly she walked to the cars with Jerry. She hated to leave for some reason. She looked back and Diane and Shane waved and she lifted her hand to them.

"Joan Vincent looked ready to collapse," said Jerry. "That's why I rushed you out of there. She needed to get back to bed."

"I wish we could help them," said Elizabeth with a sigh.

"Me, too," said Jerry. "But now, we'd better get you home before Ben starts to worry about his car."

She wrinkled her nose at Jerry; then he suddenly leaned down and gave her a quick, hard kiss on her trembling lips.

"That's another payment," he said softly, then opened Ben's car door and she slipped inside.

20

She gripped the steering wheel as she watched Jerry run to his car. She dare not let this go on! As soon as she could she'd tell him never to kiss her again.

Gently she touched her lips, then flushed and backed the car into the turnabout and drove out of the long drive to the gravel road.

Two
Ms. Kremeen

Elizabeth sat in the corner of the porch swing and watched Adam sit down beside her. Gently they pushed the swing and it creaked and Elizabeth remembered all the times she'd sat right here with Grandma Feuder and talked. "What can I do for you, Adam?"

"Just being with me these few minutes helps." He pushed his fingers through his brown curls. "Remember when I first moved in with Grandma?"

Elizabeth nodded as she once again pictured the well-dressed boy who verbally attacked everyone he met.

"I hated Grandma, then. I hated everyone." He caught Elizabeth's long, slender hand in his own, which was now brown and roughened with farm work. "Except you, Elizabeth. For some reason you understood me and loved me until finally I found God's love. With the help of Grandma and her great faith and love, he changed my life."

"What will you do now, Adam?"

He looked across the farmyard at the old barn and the chicken coop. "I want to stay right here and make this a paying farm the way it was when Grandpa was still alive."

Elizabeth smiled. "I'm glad. I thought maybe you'd sell it and move back to the city."

"I lived in the city for fourteen years and that was enough for me. I like it here. I like my neighbors." He grinned and squeezed her hand. "Especially the Johnson family."

"Thanks. I like them, too. Sometimes it's hard to remember they've only been my family since I was thirteen."

"Now you're on your way to becoming a famous concert pianist."

She laughed and flushed with pleasure. "It's a very lofty dream for a ragged, foul-mouthed aid kid to have."

"We've both come a long way, Elizabeth. I'm so glad Grandma lived long enough to hear you play in concert. She was always so proud of you. Often she'd say to me, 'That girl has what it takes to succeed. She won't give up until she has what she wants.' And she was right, Elizabeth." Adam's voice broke and tears sparkled in his dark eyes.

Elizabeth rubbed her free hand down her jeans, her cheeks pink and her hazel eyes bright with unshed tears. "I miss her, Adam. Oh, but I miss her!"

Adam nodded as he moved closer and slipped an arm lightly around her. "I am so glad you're here with me, Elizabeth. I need you. It helps just to have you beside me even if it's only for a short time."

"After all the help and encouragement that Grandma gave me, I feel I owe you support right now. She did so much for me! I want to do something in return." She stroked his cheek. "I love you, Adam."

He smiled. "And I love you. I always will. A corner of my heart will be reserved for Elizabeth Gail Johnson, concert pianist."

She laughed softly. She could smell his cologne and the fresh-air smell of him. "We'll always be friends, Adam. I may travel all over the world playing concerts, but I'll know that you're thinking of me, even praying for me. And when I come home, I'll know that you'll be right here where I can visit you."

"What dreams we have, Elizabeth." The porch swing creaked as it swayed back and forth. "Before too long I'll have cattle and pigs and chickens here on this farm along with the fields planted in corn and wheat and alfalfa. I'll fix up the place just the way Grandma always wanted to do. While I'm working I'll think of you playing to an appreciative audience, dressed up in a gorgeous gown and I'll know that you haven't forgotten me."

"I could never forget you, Adam. You're a part of my life."

"And you mine."

She pushed gently against the porch floor and set the swing in motion again. Just being with Adam made Grandma seem close.

The phone rang and Adam pushed himself up. "That might be my parents. They said they'd call when they got to Boston."

"I'll go home, Adam. See you later." They smiled farewell; then Adam hurried inside, the screen door slamming behind him.

Walking slowly to the end of the drive, she looked toward Jill Noteboom's house and sighed. Her best friend was gone for the summer. She had so much to tell Jill, but it would have to wait until Jill got home.

A pickup drove past; then Elizabeth walked along the edge of the paved road toward the Johnson farm. A hawk soared across the blue sky. The silence around her reminded her of yesterday when the car had run out of gas and she'd found Neddie.

What was he doing today? How was his mother?

Elizabeth's pace quickened. She had to do something for the Vincent family. But what? She'd told her family about them and Vera had said that she'd go help Mrs. Vincent with the kids and the house. She said that she'd take a meal to them.

Elizabeth watched a butterfly dart from wild daisy to wild daisy in the ditch. Maybe she could take Adam over and let him get acquainted with the Vincents and together they could do something. She shook her head. She wouldn't take Adam to meet them. She'd call Jerry and together they'd do something.

Once again she felt Jerry's arm tightly around her and his lips on hers. Her heart jumped; then she frowned and forced thoughts of Jerry away.

Elizabeth stopped at the mailbox and looked inside but the mail hadn't come yet. She closed the silver box, then slowly walked up the long drive. Large trees stood in the front yard. A swing hung from a branch and the grass under the swing was worn away from many years of feet kicking against the ground. A horse neighed and Elizabeth looked toward the pen beside the horse barn. Snowball stood with her white head over the top of the fence. She was waiting for Elizabeth to take her for their daily ride through the fields.

A small yellow car stood outside the garage and Elizabeth stopped and stared at it. Her mouth went dry and she clenched her fists tightly at her sides. What did Ms. Kremeen want?

Elizabeth stopped outside the back door of the house. Shivers ran up and down her spine. She frowned impatiently. How could her old caseworker still upset her this much? But why was Ms. Kremeen here?

Lunch smells still lingered in the air as Elizabeth walked down the hall toward the study. She had to find out why Ms. Kremeen was once again in the Johnsons' house. Last week she'd stopped Vera on the street in town to talk to her and Elizabeth had still felt the woman's hostility.

Elizabeth poked her head in the study and Vera looked up from Chuck's large oak desk with a smile.

"Come in, Elizabeth. Ms. Kremeen has some exciting news."

"Hello, Ms. Kremeen," said Elizabeth cautiously.

"Hello, Elizabeth." Ms. Kremeen smiled, but the smile didn't reach her cold gray eyes. Her long auburn hair was pulled back in a coil at the nape of her slender neck. She crossed her legs and smoothed her yellow skirt over her knees.

28

"Come in and sit down," said Vera, motioning for Elizabeth to take a chair. Vera's blue eyes sparkled with excitement. Blonde curls framed her face. She was dressed in light blue slacks and a white and blue knit top.

Elizabeth sat on the leather sofa and looked from Ms. Kremeen to Vera. "What's the news?"

"Ms. Kremeen wants us to take care of a baby girl for two or three weeks until the foster family that was to take her is back from vacation," explained Vera, unable to keep the pleasure from her voice. "Her name's Glorie and she's six months old."

"I'll bring her out this afternoon," said Ms. Kremeen as she stood. "Will that be convenient?"

Vera hurried around the desk. "Oh, yes! It'll be fun having a baby around again."

Elizabeth leaned back and crossed her legs. Just how much fun would it be to have a baby around? Had Vera forgotten that Scottie Johnson was coming for the next month because Gwen was going to have a baby? Scottie was ten years old so he wouldn't take quite as much time as a baby, but still he would be extra work. How could Vera find time to help the Vincent family now?

The front door closed just as the grand-father clock in the hall bonged two and

29

Elizabeth knew Ms. Kremeen was gone.

Vera hurried back in the study, laughing happily. "Last week when Ms. Kremeen suggested I take this baby for a while, I didn't think it would happen. Oh, I'm glad it did! Just think! Once again we'll set up the crib and have a baby in the house."

"And Scottie."

Vera sank down on a chair and locked her hands in her lap. "I can't believe that I forgot about Scottie coming. Luke and Gwen are bringing him tomorrow. Oh, my!" Then she shrugged. "We can manage. Kevin and Toby will take charge of Scottie, I'm sure."

"We'll really have a full house, Mom."

"I'll set the crib up in my dressing room and Scottie can sleep in the spare room." Suddenly Vera leaned forward. "Oh, Elizabeth! I forgot about the Vincent family! How can I help them now? I'm so sorry, honey! I just spread myself too thin right now."

"I'll find a way to help them, Mom." Elizabeth curled a piece of her soft hair around and around her finger. "I'll practice in the late afternoons, so I can help Mrs. Vincent during the day. I can take care of the kids and clean and fix meals." Just the thought of that much work almost took her breath away, but she smiled confidently. "I'm sure I can handle it."

"If Susan didn't have a job, she'd help."

30

Vera fingered the chain around her slender neck. "I'm sorry to go back on my word, Libby."

"That's all right, Mom. I knew I was to help the Vincent family. I felt it in my heart."

"Then the Lord will help you to know what to do." Vera smiled thoughtfully. "I know God has a special reason for me to take care of baby Glorie. I don't know what it is right now, but I'll know when the time comes."

"Baby Glorie is a lucky little girl," said Elizabeth softly.

Vera smiled, her blue eyes full of love. "Thanks, honey."

Elizabeth leaned forward earnestly. "Mom, have you ever been sorry that you adopted Toby and me?"

Vera shook her head and her blonde curls danced. "Never! Ben and Susan and Kevin were born to us, but you and Toby are just as much a part of me as they are. If I had it to do all over again, I'd still take in the little foster girl, Libby Dobbs."

Tears pricked Elizabeth's eyes. "Thanks. I couldn't have had a better mom and dad than you and Chuck. You gave me love when no one else would. I'll never forget it. I'll try my best to be what you expect me to be."

Vera moved to Elizabeth's side and took

her hands. "Honey, God has given you the talent and the desire to be a concert pianist. That's what we want for you, too. Someday you'll leave here to be on your own now that you're out of high school, but this will always be your home."

Elizabeth smiled. "Thanks, Mom. I do think I'd better go practice right now. First thing in the morning I'm going to help Mrs. Vincent. If she won't mind, I'll bring the kids here to play for a while. I know she could use the rest."

Vera hugged Elizabeth. "You're a wonderful girl."

Elizabeth wrinkled her nose. "I know."

Vera laughed and tugged Elizabeth up. "I think we'd better get you out of here before your head is too big to fit through the door."

Just then the phone rang and Elizabeth reached it first and answered. It was Jerry and she caught her breath for a moment. She held her hand over the receiver. "It's for me, Mom."

Vera lifted her hand, then walked out, closing the study door quietly.

Elizabeth leaned against the desk. "How are you, Jerry?"

"Just fine. I'm on my way to the Vincents with some food that my mom fixed. Would you like to ride over with me?"

She hesitated. If he was going to kiss her

32

again, she wouldn't. She shook her head. He'd probably just been trying to cheer her up yesterday. He wouldn't go around kissing her as if he loved her. Jerry didn't do that kind of thing. "I would like to go, Jerry. I'll be ready when you get here."

"I thought we could stay and help with dishes or whatever."

"Sounds good. See you later, Jerry." Her skin tingled as she slowly replaced the receiver. What was wrong with her? Why was she feeling so strange? So excited?

She wouldn't think about it now. Jerry would be here soon and she had to brush her hair and fix her makeup.

Would he kiss her again?

She shook her head and frowned. No! No, he certainly would not!

Three
Surprise from Jerry

Elizabeth walked toward the black Pontiac
and part of her wanted to turn and run back
into the house. Why? It was only Jerry Grosbeck, not Seth Musanto, the "handsome
stranger" she'd fallen for last summer
while she and Jill had worked for Jill's
grandmother.

"Why the frown, Elizabeth?" asked Jerry
as he held the car door open for her.

She handed him the bag of frozen food
that Vera had packed for her to take to the
Vincents and Jerry carefully set it in the
back on the floor behind the seat. The
smells of fried chicken and freshly baked
bread drifted from the car.

Elizabeth quickly cleared away the frown and smiled. "The Vincents are going to be very happy to see all of this."

Jerry nodded, then ran around and slid in under the steering wheel. He wore jeans and his long legs almost touched the black wheel. "I called them and Diane answered. She said her mother was feeling worse today, so I said we were bringing supper to them. Diane was very excited."

As they pulled out onto the road, Elizabeth watched Goosy Poosy walk away from the driveway toward the cow barn. Rex barked from where he was tied up at his doghouse. The air conditioner in the car kept the hot sun at bay.

They drove past Adam's house and she looked for him, but didn't see him.

"Adam's taking his grandma's death pretty hard," said Jerry. "I offered to help him around the place, but he said he'd make out all right."

"I plan to help Adam any way I can," she said softly, and she knew it sounded like a vow.

Jerry looked sharply at her. "Just don't do anything dumb!"

"What do you mean?"

He was quiet while he passed a state truck. "Just drop it," he said gruffly.

So she told him about baby Glorie and

how happy Vera was and Jerry's scowl disappeared.

"I admire your mom and mine." Jerry slowed, then turned onto the gravel road. "They didn't have to take in foster kids, but they did."

"Out of all the foster homes we were in, only these were full of love and caring. Someday maybe we can help kids the way our families have helped us."

The car rocked from a bump and he slowed even more. "We're living proof that two aid kids with nothing going for them can succeed. If we can do that for other kids, then part of our debt would be paid. I don't believe that we've made it this far just to forget where we came from. I feel responsible for the kids around me, kids who need help. I want them to know that since we made it, they can, too."

She smiled at him, agreeing totally with what he said. She wanted to lean across and touch the white scar that ran from the corner of his eye to his jaw. He'd told her how his dad had cut him with a broken whiskey bottle, then left him to bleed and take care of the cut as best he could. "We'll be able to do something, Jerry," she said with a catch in her voice.

"I wish that I knew what I was going to do with my life," he said hoarsely. "You're going to be a concert pianist. But what about me? Am I going to spend my entire life doing odd jobs just because I didn't get good enough grades to go to college?"

She touched his arm and he looked down, then quickly at the road ahead. "Jerry, Dad didn't have a college education and he succeeded in business. Maybe it's harder to make it, but we know it's possible."

He grinned at her. "You're right. I just feel anxious about it sometimes. Ben already has his future as a farmer all mapped out and so does Adam. But me? I'm working nights at a factory. Sure, it pays all right, but it's not what I want to do with my life." Suddenly he laughed. "Let's get off this topic before I get depressed again. With you by my side I can do anything!"

She gripped her purse tightly. What did he mean by that?

He laughed under his breath and his shoulders moved and she glared at him. Why was he laughing at her? What secret thoughts amused him?

"Relax, Libby. I'm not going to eat you."

"I never thought you were," she said stiffly.

"Didn't you?"

"Oh, just drive the car!" She stared out the window with her hands locked in her lap and her shoulders stiff. She should know by now that she couldn't get the best of Jerry Grosbeck.

"When is your next concert?"

Finally she turned from the window. "The end of the month."

"I'll make sure to buy a ticket early. One right up front."

"I'll give you one, Jerry. Don't I always?"

"But not this time." He winked at her and she frowned. "I want to buy a ticket. Next time you can give me one."

She shrugged. "If that's the way you want it."

"Are you all ready for it?"

She nodded. "I've been practicing for it for a while now."

Jerry slowed, then pulled around a tractor. "Sometimes I wish that you weren't so talented."

"Why?" Her eyes flew open wide and she stared at him as if he'd lost his mind.

"Your piano gets more of your time than I do." He kept his eyes straight ahead and she saw him grip the steering wheel tighter. "I want more of your time and attention. I want to take you out or just sit and talk to you." He glanced at her and his eyes were full of anguish. "Will you make time for me?"

"Oh, Jerry!" She wanted to cry. "How can I give up my piano? I've worked too long and too hard to give it up now."

He shook his head and his hair fell over his wide forehead. "I don't want you to give it up. I just want you to squeeze me in. I need you to!"

She heard the urgency in his voice and she bit her bottom lip. Before she could think of something to say, he stopped in the Vincents' driveway and the three kids and a dog ran to the car.

"Our welcoming committee," said Jerry with a chuckle.

Elizabeth had barely touched her feet to the sandy drive when Neddie flung himself at her. He wrapped his thin arms around her legs and almost tipped her over. She laughed and pried him loose and lifted him to her hip. His tee shirt and shorts were dirty, as well as his face and hands. He kissed her wetly on the cheek and she hugged him tighter.

"How's Neddie?"

"Did you bring ice cream?"

"We'll ask Jerry." Elizabeth laughed and set Neddie on the ground. "Jerry, did you bring ice cream?"

"Let me think." He tipped his head and rested one finger on the side of his nose. "Did I bring ice cream?"

"Yes!" shouted Diane and Shane together, jumping up and down.

"Yes!" cried Jerry, throwing his hands wide.

"Vanilla and chocolate swirl. And fried chicken and escalloped potatoes. Shall I go on?"

"I'm hungry," said Shane, tugging at his shaggy brown hair. "Diane only fixed beans for lunch." He wrinkled his small nose.

"So what?" cried Diane, standing with her feet apart, her fists on her hips. "You ate them, didn't you?"

"Hey, let's get this stuff in the house," said Elizabeth. She lifted out the bag of frozen food and it felt icy against her arms and hands.

Several minutes later they had the food taken care of and Elizabeth walked in to talk to Joan Vincent.

Joan sat up in bed and clutched a worn robe around her. Her blue eyes had dark circles around them and her hair was dirty and tangled. "I really can't let you and Jerry do this for us, Elizabeth," Joan said weakly.

"Yes, you can, Mrs. Vincent."

"Please. Call me Joan." She rubbed her head and took a deep breath. "I don't know why I'm having such a hard time carrying this baby. I didn't have any trouble with the others."

"Have you seen a doctor?"

She nodded. "He says that I have toxic poisoning and that I must stay off my feet as much as possible. The kids are good about helping, but they are so little!"

41

"You can stop fretting. Jerry and I are going to help you as much as we can. And I know if the church ladies knew about your problem, they'd be right out to help, too."

"But they hardly know us! You hardly know us!"

Elizabeth smiled and shrugged. "What time does your husband get home?"

"David usually comes in about five, but sometimes he works later and doesn't get here until six or seven."

"If it's all right, we'll feed the kids and get them bathed. Then you and your husband can eat together in here."

"I can make it to the table with help. Oh, but I hate to see you doing all of this!"

"It's all right, Joan. I want to. Just relax and take a nap and Jerry and I will take care of everything."

Joan slowly sank back on the pillow and closed her eyes. Elizabeth looked quickly around the room and decided that while Joan was eating later, she'd come in and clean.

Much later Elizabeth walked wearily to the car with Jerry. The sun was low in the sky and had lost part of its heat.

"You did a wonderful job in there, Elizabeth," said Jerry as he opened the car door for her. "After Neddie's bath, I didn't recognize him. And they really enjoyed the food."

She sank in the seat and leaned her head back and smiled up at him. "You had the kitchen shining. You'll make a fine housekeeper someday."

He tugged one of her curls and laughed, then closed her door and walked around the front of the car. She watched him and he still looked full of energy. He smelled like the lemony dish soap he'd used in the kitchen.

"I told Joan that we'd be back about nine in the morning," said Elizabeth with a tired sigh. "I don't know if I can handle that."

"Sure you can." Jerry drove out of the drive and turned toward home. "You can do anything you put your mind to."

"Thanks a lot." She made a face and he laughed. Suddenly she thought of Adam and how lonely he was and she sighed. She turned toward Jerry. "I had a nice talk with Adam today."

"And?"

"He's so lonely, so sad. I want to comfort him. I wish I could think of something that I could do to help him."

With a sharp turn Jerry pulled into a drive that led into an alfalfa field. He turned to Elizabeth, his face blank. "Are you falling in love with Adam?"

"Me? What a silly thing to say!"

"I saw your face when you talked about him. I heard what you said. I've patiently waited for four years for you to wake up and notice that I'm alive, and what do you do? You turn to Adam just because he lost his grandma and you feel sorry for him. And feeling sorry for him can lead to deeper feelings. You are not going to fall for Adam Feuder!"

"Just who do you think you are, Jerry Grosbeck?" Oh, she couldn't believe her ears!

"I mean it, Elizabeth. I won't allow you to fall for Adam!"

Anger flared in her and her hazel eyes flashed. "And what do you have to do with it?"

Jerry turned from her and gripped the steering wheel until his knuckles were white. Finally he looked at her and she met his gaze unflinchingly. "I know that you have special feelings for me!"

"What?" she shrieked. "When did you get so arrogant?"

"It's the truth."

She clamped her mouth closed tightly and stared straight ahead at two birds flying low over the field.

Jerry rubbed a finger down her cheek and she jerked away as if it had burned her. He cleared his throat. "Be honest with yourself, Elizabeth. Don't be afraid to admit that you care about me."

Oh, the nerve of the guy! "Take me home right now," she said grimly.

"You know I'm telling it the way it is."

"Loving you is not part of my life's plan!"

Pain crossed his face, then was gone. "For two summers I let you have your own way. I kept quiet while you fell in love. I kept quiet week after week when you got letters and phone calls from those guys. Do you know how much that hurt me? Do you know how I suffered? Well, I'm not going to do that any longer. I love you and I always will! I'm going to do everything I can do to make you admit that you love me."

"It won't do any good."

"I'll take that chance."

"Oh, Jerry! You are absolutely impossible!"

"You *do* love me!"

She pushed open the car door and almost fell out. She turned and glared at him. "I'll walk home! You can just take yourself and your crazy love talk and get out of my life! I didn't ask for any of this."

He was beside her in a flash and she looked wildly around for a place to run to escape him, but she knew he could run faster. He gripped her arms and shook her, then held her quietly, looking down at her for several minutes.

"Forget the whole thing, Elizabeth. Get in the car and I'll take you home."

"Let me go," she whispered fiercely.

"Will you run away?"

She hesitated, then shook her head. His hands were burning into her arms and her stomach fluttered strangely. "Let me go, Jerry. Please."

Abruptly he released her, then strode back around the car.

Slowly she slid in and huddled as close to the passenger door as she could. She wanted to look at him to see how much she'd hurt him but she kept her eyes straight ahead, her chin high.

Four
The softball game

Elizabeth sat at her desk and rubbed the
puzzle box that her real dad had sent her for
her twelfth birthday. But she wasn't thinking
of Frank Dobbs or that he'd died and left her
a part of Sandhill Ranch. She was thinking
of Jerry and what he'd said to her and how
she'd worked side by side with him for
several days even though she'd been very
upset with him.

Why had he ruined everything for them
with that silly talk about love? Elizabeth
pushed the puzzle box back and looked
around the pink, dark pink, and red
bedroom. Once Jerry had walked in here to

look around so that he could see how she lived. He'd said that it pleased him to think that she had a beautiful room instead of the shabby rooms she'd had while she was being kicked from foster home to foster home. Why did he even care? Why had he said he loved her?

She rammed her fingers through her curls and pressed her head tightly. Why did Jerry think that *she* loved *him?* Well, she certainly did not!

She paced the floor, stepping around the large round red hassock. If this kept up, she'd never be able to practice for the concert with any amount of concentration. She stopped and laced her fingers together and breathed deeply.

Her stomach grumbled with hunger. For the past several days she'd only picked at her food. Sunday dinner today had stuck in her throat. With Scottie and baby Glorie taking all the attention, no one had commented on her lack of appetite.

She glanced at her watch, then frowned. Jerry would be here soon to play ball. She'd heard Ben invite him this morning after church. He had glanced quickly at her, then agreed happily to play softball with the Johnson family.

With icy hands she tucked her tee shirt into her jeans. She didn't want to play ball with Jerry around. Maybe Adam would make it back in time so she could use him as a barrier between herself and Jerry.

She jerked open her door. She certainly didn't need someone to protect her from Jerry. She was a big girl now and well able to take care of herself. Besides, he wouldn't talk any foolish love talk with her whole family standing around. Would he? She rubbed her cheek nervously as she walked down the hall toward the open stairway.

"Wait for me, Elizabeth."

She turned at the top of the stairs and smiled at Susan. Even in an old tee shirt and faded jeans Susan looked as if she was ready to reign as Miss America. Her red gold hair hung in two long braids down her slender shoulders and her blue eyes sparkled with happiness. Elizabeth felt tall and awkward and plain next to Susan.

"I'm glad it's not too hot to play ball today," said Susan with a merry laugh. "I told Scottie he could be on our team. I hope you don't mind."

"Not at all," said Elizabeth as she walked downstairs with Susan. The grandfather clock ticked loudly, the brass pendulum slowly swinging back and forth. "It'll make the game more exciting and interesting." As long as Jerry wasn't on their side. Oh, she must stop thinking about Jerry!

Susan stopped near the back door. "Isn't it funny, Libby, that Aunt Gwen used to be

49

your Miss Miller? Now she and Uncle Luke are going to have a baby."

Elizabeth nodded as she thought of all the years Miss Miller had come for her when she was in trouble in a foster home or with Mother. Miss Miller always helped her and she finally found this home for her. "I remember when I first met Uncle Luke and Scottie. It was when I went to stay with Grandma and Grandpa Johnson during spring vacation when I was twelve. Scottie was four and he saw Miss Miller and wanted her for his mother."

"And Uncle Luke had already met Miss Miller and had loved her, then lost her. He married Aunt Bea and she died; then he found Miss Miller and they got married and lived happily ever after."

Elizabeth jabbed Susan's arm. "Oh, Susan, you think everything is so romantic!" Elizabeth laughed and Susan joined in as they walked out into the warm afternoon.

Rex barked and Goosy Poosy honked from the chicken pen where he was locked for the afternoon so that he wouldn't try to play softball with the family.

"Sorry, Goosy Poosy," said Susan as they walked past the pen. "We don't have a bat your size."

"We should ask Toby to make one for him," said Elizabeth with a laugh. "Toby's fifteen years old but I'll bet he'd still take

Goosy Poosy to his bedroom if Mom would let him."

Just then a car pulled into the drive and the girls turned to look and Susan said excitedly, "Look! It's Jerry! I'm so glad he came!"

Elizabeth looked wildly around for a place to hide. She wasn't ready to talk to Jerry yet. "You go meet him, Susan. I'll tell the others you're on your way. We sure don't want to keep the game waiting." She sounded breathless and she hated it. Her face flushed red and perspiration dotted her forehead. Did Susan notice how strange she was acting?

Susan dashed toward the black Pohtiac, her braids flying out behind her. She caught Jerry's arm and Elizabeth bit her bottom lip as a pang of jealousy shot through her. Abruptly she turned and half ran toward the playing field. She could hear shouts and laughter. Scottie called to her, then ran to her side, his red gold hair bouncing. He looked like a combination of Kevin and Susan, close enough to be a brother instead of a cousin.

"I'm on your side, Libby!" Scottie said, grinning up at her. He was dressed in new jeans and a light blue tee shirt with one pocket. He had a mitt on his left hand and he kept hitting it with his right fist. "Come on! Are you ready to play?"

"Almost, Scottie." She smiled down at

him and suddenly remembered another Scott that she knew, Scott Norris. She'd fallen in love with him when she was thirteen and he was nineteen. She turned her head and laughed to herself. She had thought she'd love him forever but now he was married to Cousin Rhonda and they were very happy.

"Here comes Susan!" Scottie dashed toward Susan and Jerry and Elizabeth glanced at them, then looked again. Jerry was holding Susan's hand!

Her heart raced and her head spun. How could he hold Susan's hand when he said that he loved her? But maybe he'd been teasing. He always teased her. Oh, but she'd be angry if he'd put her through all this misery just to tease her! She doubled her fists and took a deep breath.

"Play ball!" shouted Chuck from home plate.

Elizabeth rubbed her hands down her jeans as she walked through the grass that was kept mowed just for ball games. She glanced at Jerry and he nodded and said hello and she lifted her head higher and said hello in what she hoped was an icy voice. She shot a look at his hand holding Susan's and he saw it and his broad shoulders moved in silent laughter and she clenched her fists. He was really asking for it! Well, she'd get him by playing so well that his side lost and then she'd see just how much he laughed!

Chuck's side won first play and Elizabeth stood beside Scottie waiting her turn to bat. Those on Ben's side took their places and Jerry stopped at the pitcher's mound and Elizabeth's heart sank. How could she bat with Jerry as pitcher? She rubbed her hands up and down her arms and tried to think of a way to get out of playing ball, but she knew she couldn't. Many Sunday afternoons were spent playing ball and today Kevin and Toby had asked some of their friends over to even up the sides.

Finally Elizabeth picked up the bat and stood ready for the pitch. She tried not to look at Jerry, but he was smiling at her as if she was the light of his life.

"Hit me a pop fly, sweetheart," shouted Jerry and Elizabeth wanted to sink out of sight. What would her family think?

He pitched and she swung, determined to hit a home run. The swing almost knocked her off balance.

"Don't give up, darling," he called with a wink.

She tapped the plate with the tip of her bat. "Just pitch, will you?" Her hands felt damp and slippery on the bat.

He pitched and again she swung and missed. Her temper rose and her cheeks flushed red and perspiration dotted her forehead. Why was Jerry pitcher, of all things?

"Don't strike out," called Susan from first base where she stood poised to run to second.

Jerry pitched and Elizabeth swung and missed and she dropped the bat and marched away from the plate.

"Don't take it so hard," said Chuck softly as Scottie stood up to bat. "You'll do better next time."

"Thanks, Dad. Jerry's been teasing me and he got me all messed up." She forced a smile and Chuck squeezed her shoulder.

"Jerry's a fine boy," said Chuck. "Once he knows where he's going in life, he'll make it."

Scottie hit the ball and ran toward first while Susan ran to second. Vera stood on the sidelines with Glorie in her arms, shouting for Susan and Scottie.

"I don't know what to make of Jerry sometimes," said Elizabeth softly. "Sometimes I feel I don't even know him, yet I've known him for years and years."

Chuck pushed his fingers through his red hair. Laugh lines spread from the corners of his hazel eyes to his gray temples. "We all change, Elizabeth. Look how much you've changed in the past few years. We have to stay close enough to our family and friends to keep acquainted with them. You love Jerry."

Her stomach tightened.

"You have loved him for years and you know he's worth keeping as a dear friend. Since you spend time with him at the Vincents, talk to him and listen to him and get to know him the way he is now in this point in his life."

"Thanks, Dad. You're always there when I need you."

Suddenly the bat cracked against the ball and the ball flew across the field and Tim Murphy, one of Toby's friends, shouted with victory as he ran toward first, then on. Susan and Scottie came in; then Tim slid into home and Elizabeth leaped high and shouted with the others on her team.

By the time the game was over and Chuck's team had won, Elizabeth felt hot and sweaty and was ready for the iced tea that she knew Vera had waiting for everyone at the picnic table near the back of the house.

Elizabeth rubbed her damp face and lifted her hair off her neck and let the breeze cool her off. When Jerry fell into step beside her she was able to smile up at him. "You only struck me out once, Jerry. I hope you noticed that."

He grinned and shrugged. "There's always another day." He laid his arm across her shoulders and her stomach fluttered, but she didn't shrug him away. Just now she liked the weight of his arm around her. "But I must admit that you all played a good game."

She smiled up at him, then looked quickly away from the warm light in his eyes. "Your team played very well, too, just not quite good enough."

"We'll get Scottie on our team next time and then we'll be sure to win. That little guy can really play."

Elizabeth agreed as she watched Scottie talking excitedly to Toby and his friends as they crowded around the picnic table for snacks and drinks.

Snowball neighed from the pen near the horse barn and Elizabeth turned with a laugh. "I think Snowball feels left out."

"Let's go talk to her," said Jerry, leading Elizabeth across the grassy yard to the horse pen. "We can't have your mare feeling left out."

"It's hard to believe she's been mine since I was twelve years old and she wasn't much bigger than the foal beside her." Elizabeth patted Snowball's neck. The white foal pushed her nose through the fence and Elizabeth stroked it gently.

"Elizabeth, I wanted a chance to talk privately to you," said Jerry in a low, tense voice.

She backed away. "Why?" Had she made a mistake by walking alone with him?

He pushed his fingers through his brown

hair, his lids down to cover the expression in his dark eyes. Finally he looked into her watchful eyes. "I want you to stay away from Adam Feuder."

"What?"

"You heard me." A muscle jumped in his jaw and the scar on his face stood out boldly against his dark skin.

"Don't be ridiculous!"

"Please, Elizabeth. For me."

"Will you stop this right now, Jerry?"

The bleak look in his eyes surprised her. "I just don't know you, Libby. I thought I did. I thought you'd be able to see what you're doing and stop it."

She lifted her pointed chin a fraction higher. "Stop what?"

He gripped her arms and his fingers bit into her flesh. "With Adam! You can't fall in love with him. You belong with me and you always have and always will!"

Her pulse leaped and for one wild minute she wanted to lean against him and feel his arms close around her and his lips press against hers. Then reason returned and she stiffened. "Let me go, Jerry Grosbeck! I thought we were friends, but we certainly won't be if you continue acting this way!"

"We're more than friends, Elizabeth Gail Johnson!" He pulled her hard against himself and kissed her. She struggled weakly, then relaxed against him. Her fingers curled into his shirt front and her heart leaped wildly.

He finally lifted his head and looked into her flushed face. He smiled. "You find Adam and tell him you can't see him again."

She jerked back, her eyes flashing. "You'll do anything to get your own way, won't you? You didn't kiss me because you care about me! Adam needs me. I won't desert him. You can't change my mind with a few kisses!"

His face darkened. "You are impossible! I don't know why I bother with you!"

"I don't either! I certainly never asked you to."

He glared at her, then strode to his car and drove away. She leaned weakly against the fence and Snowball nuzzled her shoulder.

"Why do I have to fight with him, Snowball?" she whispered tearfully.

Five
Big decision

Abruptly Elizabeth turned and walked into
the cool, dimly lit horse barn. Tears stung
her eyes and she blinked them rapidly away
as she walked slowly to a bale of hay and sat
down. The pungent odor was pleasant to her
and the silence relaxed her a little. A barn
cat slept in a shaft of sunlight on a bale of
hay. Elizabeth watched as its ear twitched to
chase away a fly. She wished she felt that
peaceful. The dust tickled her nose and she
sneezed, then sneezed again. She rubbed her
nose with the back of her hand, then leaned
back against a pile of baled hay. What was
she going to do about Jerry Grosbeck?

Elizabeth folded her arms and rocked forward and backward, forward and back. She would not scream or shout! Jerry Grosbeck couldn't make her that upset!

The barn door opened and someone blocked the door. Elizabeth sniffed hard and knuckled away more tears.

"Elizabeth, is something wrong?" Susan walked slowly to the bales of hay, then stood looking down at Elizabeth's bent head.

"I'm fine," Elizabeth said stiffly.

"I saw Jerry drive out."

"Did you?" Elizabeth wanted to run and not stop until she was too exhausted to think or feel.

"I saw him kiss you." Susan leaned against a support post.

"I don't want to talk about it!"

Susan shook her head, then pushed her hands into her jeans pockets. "I don't know why you and Jerry have such a hard time, Elizabeth. I tried to help you when you were away at music camp and he was here eating his heart out. I couldn't take it then and I can't take it now. He looks at me with those sad brown eyes and I almost burst into tears. He loves you, Elizabeth, and I think you love him. Why do you push him away?"

Elizabeth jumped up, her fists doubled at her sides. "Susan, leave me alone! I didn't appreciate your interference before and I don't now!"

60

"I only want to help." Susan sounded as if she'd burst into tears and Elizabeth's anger melted.

"I know, Susan, but you can't. It's between Jerry and me. We'll work it out. I think I'll have to stop seeing him altogether."

"But you see him every day at the Vincents'."

Elizabeth's hazel eyes flashed. "Then I'll stop going to the Vincents'! And I'll make sure that I'm not home when he comes here to visit!"

Susan clicked her tongue. "You're trying too hard. That must tell you something."

"It tells me that I'm going to start hating him if he doesn't leave me alone!" Oh, if he were here right now she'd let him know just what she thought and felt!

Susan laughed softly. "Elizabeth, don't lie to yourself. It doesn't help at all."

"You don't know what you're talking about." Elizabeth pushed damp hair off her cheek. Why didn't Susan leave her alone? She was not lying to herself!

"I know what I see, Elizabeth," said Susan softly but firmly. "And I know that you care deeply for Jerry. You've always had special feelings for him and I think it's because you both went through so much while you were foster children."

Elizabeth sighed. She watched a spider

61

swing from the corner of a post to the wall. Snowball nickered outside the barn. "I guess I do love Jerry, Susan, but it's not the kind of love you mean."

"And how do you know that?" Susan stood with her head tipped, her hands on her narrow waist.

"Let's drop it, Susan! I'm tired of thinking about and talking about Jerry Grosbeck. Right now I'm going inside to take a shower and change so I can practice." She strode toward the door and Susan ran after her and caught her arm and she stopped with a frown.

"Give Jerry a chance. He's a special guy. He's absolutely wonderful!"

Elizabeth clenched her fists and her nails bit into her palms as she once again thought of Susan and Jerry holding hands, smiling at each other in a special way. Impatiently she pushed open the barn door and stepped into the late afternoon sunlight. She blinked hard. "Drop it, Susan! I am tired of talking about Jerry!" Was Susan falling in love with Jerry? But that couldn't be. Susan was going with Randy Grayson.

Just then a car drove in and Elizabeth lifted her head and her heart leaped as she saw Adam. She ran toward the driveway and reached the car just as Adam slid out. She flung herself into his arms and gave him a quick hug. He studied her with his warm brown eyes that suddenly seemed very much like Jerry's. She lowered her eyes and he lifted her chin and forced her to look at him.

"I can tell that something is wrong. What is it, Elizabeth?"

"I'm just glad to see you," she said breathlessly. *He'd* never mess up their relationship by falling in love with her.

"I can tell there's more to it than that."

She wanted to tell him about Jerry, but her throat closed over and she shrugged.

"I had a fine dinner and a wonderful visit with the Brakie twins and their family," Adam continued. "It was very nice of April and May to ask me over for the day. They know how lonely I get without Grandma."

"They're good friends." She walked with him across the front yard and he stopped her near the swing. She rubbed the rope and he showed her a large fox squirrel on the branch of another tree.

"Did you practice yet, Elizabeth?"

She shook her head. "I was on my way in just now."

"I suppose that means that I can't take you away for a while."

She sighed. "I don't have time. I'm sorry."

He shrugged with a grin. "I'll see if Ben wants to come over later for a game of chess."

"I don't think he has a date tonight."

Elizabeth sat on the worn board and gripped the ropes and Adam pushed her slowly.

"I haven't seen you much lately, Elizabeth. How soon is Joan Vincent's baby due?"

"Two weeks, maybe a little more." Elizabeth watched a robin hop across the grass that Kevin and Toby kept mowed. "I'm thinking about staying home tomorrow."

"You are?" Adam stopped the swing and looked down into her face. "Is something wrong? Or is someone else going to help her?"

Why couldn't she just tell him how she felt about going with Jerry? "I do need to get in more practice, Adam. I don't want to mess up on a concert."

He grinned and shook his head. "You won't. Maybe you should go in now. I don't want to take up your practice time."

"Don't leave yet!" The urgency in her voice made her flush and she saw his sudden questioning look. She forced a laugh. "You've only just come. I'd like you to stay longer." With him near her it was easier to stop thinking about Jerry.

"I would like to, but I won't take up your valuable practice time. You're busy enough without me taking your time." His brown hand squeezed her shoulder and he turned and walked toward his car.

Abruptly she turned and walked to the house. She wouldn't think about Adam or Jerry right now. She had to practice her piano. Once at the piano there wouldn't be room for anything else in her mind. It had to be that way or she'd fail as a concert pianist.

Later as she sat at the piano she made mistake after mistake and finally she jumped up and paced from the fireplace to the piano to the couch and back. She could hear the others in different parts of the house and she wanted to join them and forget about practicing or thinking or anything. She stopped at the piano bench and looked at the music on the piano. She'd played the sonata dozens of times. Why couldn't she now?

Vera poked her head in, baby Glorie in her arms. "Anything wrong, Elizabeth?"

"Oh, Mom! I can't get this sonata!"

Vera bent to look at the music with Glorie pressed against her shoulder. Glorie looked around with bright blue eyes. Her head was almost bald and she was dressed in a pink shirt and a diaper.

"You've played this before, Elizabeth. You shouldn't have trouble with it." Vera sat down on the couch with Glorie. "Is something troubling you, Elizabeth?"

Elizabeth sat on the bench and leaned forward with her hands between her knees.

"Mom, I'm going to have to quit helping Joan Vincent. I can't let anything stand in the way of my practice."

"I probably could go myself tomorrow if you can watch Glorie and Scottie."

Elizabeth grabbed at that and it felt as if a heavy weight had been lifted off her shoulders. "Thanks, Mom! I think that would help me a lot."

Vera laid Glorie across her legs and smiled as the baby cooed and gurgled. "I don't know if Ms. Kremeen is coming tomorrow or not. She said she might."

"She still hates me, Mom."

Vera smiled. "That's her problem and not yours. When Ms. Kremeen thinks she's right, she goes all out to get her own way." Vera patted Glorie. "Ms. Kremeen is determined to keep this baby away from her natural mother. She said that the mother will try anything to get Glorie back. Ms. Kremeen is just as determined to keep the baby from her."

Elizabeth shook her head. "Just for that reason alone I'd like to see Glorie with her real mother. Ms. Kremeen doesn't have good judgment."

Vera smiled. "That might not be true all the time, Elizabeth. She was wrong about you, but if she was wrong all the time she wouldn't be able to keep her job."

66

"I guess you're right."

Glorie opened her mouth and cried and Vera stood up and said she had to change Glorie's diaper. She smiled encouragingly at Elizabeth as they left the room. The crying grew fainter and fainter and then Elizabeth couldn't hear it.

She stood at the window and looked out. Soon the sun would be down. Tomorrow she'd be able to stay home and keep away from Jerry. Her stomach tightened and an uneasy feeling pressed in on her. Was she doing the right thing by staying home tomorrow?

She walked to the couch and sank down on the edge and wrapped her hands around her knees. God had put the Vincent family on her heart so that she'd help them. His plan for her hadn't changed.

She sighed and shook her head. How could she step out of God's will for her just because of her feelings toward Jerry?

With a sigh she covered her face with her hands. "Heavenly Father, forgive me. I do want to do what you want me to do. I will continue to help the Vincent family until the job is done. Help me to deal with Jerry with your help and your love."

Finally Elizabeth lifted her head and managed to smile. Things would work out just fine. She wasn't alone and she never would be. Somehow she'd find a way to tell Jerry to leave her alone. She didn't want his love.

A great loneliness engulfed her and she leaned back on the couch. Hot tears stung her eyes, then slowly slipped down her pale cheeks.

Six
Mrs. Briggs
and the Vincents

Scottie suddenly leaned against the front car
seat and poked his head between Jerry and
Elizabeth. "Are you sure they'll like me? I
never played with twins before."

Elizabeth glanced out of the corner of her
eye at Jerry as he assured Scottie that the
Vincent children would love him.

Elizabeth gripped her purse in her lap. Did
Jerry know that she'd brought Scottie along
this morning just so she wouldn't have to be
alone with him? She moistened her dry lips
with the tip of her tongue. Was he silently
laughing at her?

"You can help me weed the garden,
Scottie," said Jerry as he slowed to turn into
the Vincents' drive.

Scottie groaned and slumped in his seat, then bobbed forward. "Will Diane and Shane help, too?"

"They always do," answered Jerry as he stopped the car near the rundown garage.

Elizabeth slipped out of the car and looked around the yard with a pleased smile. Jerry had worked a miracle in the yard and David Vincent had praised him over and over for it, then thanked him over and over.

The smile faded and Elizabeth looked around apprehensively. Where were the kids and the dog that always met them the minute they drove in? Was something wrong? She rushed to the door and opened it . . . and walked in to find Diane in tears.

"What's wrong?" asked Elizabeth softly as she wiped the tears off Diane's pale face.

"Grandma's coming and we made a mess and can't get it cleaned up before she gets here." Diane's thin shoulders shook with her crying and giant tears rolled from her blue eyes. "Mom's trying to clean and she hurts too much, but she won't go back to bed!"

Elizabeth stifled a cry of alarm as she rushed to the kitchen where she heard dishes clattering. Joan stood at the sink, her face white and puffy, her shoulders stooped.

"Joan, I'll do that," said Elizabeth firmly. "You go back to bed before you hurt yourself."

Joan looked up and tears filled her eyes

70

that were so much like Diane's. "I have to hurry. Mom is coming in an hour and she'll see the house is a mess." Joan touched her hair and plucked at her sleeve. "And I need a bath and a change of clothes!"

Elizabeth gripped Joan's arm and led her to a kitchen chair and helped her down into it. "Joan, Jerry and I will take care of everything. We really will. You rest a minute, then take a shower and wash your hair. You get yourself ready and we'll see to the house and the kids."

"She didn't want us to move to the country." Joan locked her hands together on the table. "She said we had no business moving so far away from her. She hasn't been here for two months and she doesn't know that I'm sick. But she's coming this morning! Oh, dear!"

"Just relax, Joan. We'll have everything looking good. I brought a coffee cake that Susan baked early this morning. I'll make coffee and serve the coffee cake."

Joan clutched Elizabeth's wrist. "Oh, but you can't be here when she comes! I don't want her to know I had to accept charity from anyone!"

"But this isn't charity. I'm helping you out just as you'd help someone in trouble."

"She won't see it that way and I'll never hear the end of it!"

Elizabeth frowned thoughtfully. "We

brought Scottie with us today. We'll let your mom think that we came over just for Scottie to play with the twins. She doesn't have to know that we helped you get ready for her visit."

Joan sighed as she chewed her bottom lip. Finally she nodded. "All right, Elizabeth. I'll go bathe and leave you with all the dirty work."

"It's not very messed up in here so it won't take long at all."

Joan brushed away her tears, then awkwardly stood up and walked away. Elizabeth rushed to the back door and flung it wide.

"Jerry! Scottie! I need you now!"

Jerry ran to the door and grabbed her arms and looked anxiously into her face. "What's the matter?"

She saw his concern and for some strange reason it pleased her. She shook her head. "It's all right, Jerry. I just need you both to come in and help me in here awhile."

"Where are the kids?" asked Scottie with a frown as he looked around the small kitchen.

Elizabeth squeezed his shoulder. "They're cleaning their bedrooms. Let's sit down and make plans before we do anything else."

Jerry gave her a quick, sharp look, then sat at the table and leaned his elbows on the

Formica tabletop. "Give us our orders, boss."

Elizabeth laughed as she sank to a chair. "Joan's mother is coming to visit in a few minutes and she's very fussy, so Joan wants everything just right. And she doesn't want her mother to know that we've been coming to help out. I said that we'd follow her wishes, so for today we're only visitors. But first we must all work together to put the house in order." She took a deep breath. "Scottie, will you help the kids as much as you can? After we're finished, I promise that you can play with them."

"I'll help." Scottie shook his head and his red gold hair bounced. "I can clean good."

"Me, too," said Jerry with a serious look, then a wink. "Where shall I start?"

All Elizabeth's anger and apprehension toward Jerry melted away and she smiled and pushed herself up and quickly assigned the work for herself as well as Jerry.

"I'll take Scottie to meet the kids," said Jerry as he motioned for Scottie to follow him.

Elizabeth watched them walk away and a little bubble of laughter burst out. Why did she feel so excited about being with Jerry if she didn't love him? She frowned and pushed the disturbing thought away. She had work to do. She couldn't stand here looking after Jerry as if he was the light of her life.

Quickly she cleared off the table and washed it, then rubbed it dry until it shone. She washed off the stove and refrigerator and finished the dishes.

Jerry rushed in and grabbed her and swung her around and she laughed breathlessly. "What next?" he asked as he released her. "I'm ready to go!"

"Did you finish the other room?" Just being near him sent her pulse racing and she stepped back and bumped into the counter near the stove.

He nodded. "And Joan is sitting on the couch all clean and ready. I sent the kids out to play in the yard with orders to stay clean."

"Thanks. I'm so glad that you're here!"

He leaned toward her and she could smell the furniture polish that he'd used. "I am so thankful that you're you. You're absolutely fantastic and wonderful as well as gorgeous."

She flushed with pleasure. "Thank you. But we'd better stop talking and fix the coffee and the cake and go to the living room and sit down. Joan's mother will be here very soon."

Jerry held his hand out to her and she hesitated, then slipped her hand in his. Shivers of excitement ran up and down her spine. Her eyes met his and she felt pinned to the spot.

He cleared his throat. "Yes, well, we'd better go."

"Yes," she whispered huskily.

Joan looked up with a smile as they walked in and sat in chairs across from the couch. Joan's hair was a medium blonde now that it was clean and it fluffed prettily around her face. She was dressed in blue slacks and a blue and white maternity top. She looked relaxed and rested. "I am not going to worry. You and the children have the place looking very good. Mom will complain, but that's just her way. I hope she'll see that we are happy living in the country. I want the kids to enjoy having a grandma."

"I hear a car," said Jerry.

Joan gasped and her face turned almost as white as the drapes at the windows. "Oh, dear!"

"I'll bring in the coffee, Joan. You just relax and Jerry will answer the door." Elizabeth hurried to the kitchen and quickly fixed the tray with coffee and cake. She'd already put saucers and forks with cream and sugar and cups on the tray. Carefully she carried it in and set it on the end table between the chairs that she and Jerry had sat in. She turned as Jerry opened the door. A short, plump woman with gray hair walked in, then stopped and looked suspiciously at Elizabeth.

"Come in, Mom," said Joan from the couch. "I'm sorry that I can't get up, but I do have to stay off my feet." She introduced Elizabeth and Jerry, then asked her mother to sit down for coffee.

"Here's a cup of coffee for you, Mrs. Briggs," said Elizabeth as she held out a cup on a yellow saucer.

Mrs. Briggs hesitated, then took the cup and asked for cream. She sat back and studied Joan. "I am surprised that you have friends out here this far from town, Joan. I don't want to be rude, but I did come to visit you." She looked at Elizabeth and Jerry. "Do you mind if I talk to my daughter alone?"

Elizabeth looked helplessly at Joan and she nodded. "We'll be outdoors with the kids."

Jerry held the door open and she walked out and breathed deeply. It would be easier with the kids. She looked at Jerry and rolled her eyes.

"I can see why Joan was worried."

Jerry laughed. "But she'll be all right. Let's take the kids for a walk. I told them I would and this seems to be a good time."

"I am so glad that I was here to help today!" She thought about her plans yesterday to get out of coming and she shivered. Joan had needed her today. Vera wouldn't have been able to do as much so quickly since she didn't know the house.

They walked slowly toward the kids. "I'm glad, too," said Jerry softly. "I must admit that it's not always easy to take time to come here, but I know this is what the Lord wants of me, so I do it."

Just then Neddie ran across the yard and grabbed Elizabeth around the legs, almost upsetting her. She laughed and swung Neddie into her arms. He laughed and his face was flushed and his eyes sparkled.

"Did you bring me candy?" asked Neddie.

"Not today, but I did bring a cake. After a while we'll go inside and have a piece."

"I want cake now," said Neddie, struggling to get down.

"Right now we're going for a walk," said Jerry. He called to Diane and Shane and Scottie and they ran to him eagerly.

Elizabeth lowered Neddie to the grass and he pushed through Shane and Scottie and grabbed Jerry's jean-clad leg. Elizabeth smiled as she remembered Jerry when he was Shane's age. Now Jerry was grown and happy and helping others. Being ragged foster kids together suddenly seemed a long way off. The tall, lean boy with the scar on his face was a very different boy from the one who had stolen the food from her plate so that he wouldn't go hungry.

She walked with them and listened to

Jerry tell stories about woodland creatures and show the kids footprints and homes for animals.

Suddenly he looked at her and smiled and the whole world stood still. Finally he looked away and she could breathe again. Her heart thudded so loud she was sure he could hear it. She shook her head hard. It didn't mean anything. Not anything at all!

Seven
Regina and Glorie

Elizabeth walked listlessly from the family room to the kitchen, then picked a dead leaf off a plant hanging at the kitchen window. With everyone gone tonight, the house was very quiet. Too quiet. It gave her too much time to think. She frowned and absently dabbed up a water spot with a dishtowel. Maybe she shouldn't have volunteered to baby-sit with Glorie so the family could go out together.

Her glance strayed to the phone and she looked quickly away. She would not think about Jerry calling her! She didn't want him to call. The strange feelings she'd had today wouldn't last. He wasn't *that* important to her. She wouldn't let that happen.

She rubbed the back of a kitchen chair. Maybe she should call Adam and talk to him.

The front door bell chimed and she jumped, her hands suddenly icy, her heart racing. Was it Jerry? Would he come tonight to see her, to take advantage of her softening toward him today? Excitement feathered over her and a smile tugged at her mouth. Maybe that's what she needed—to know her own heart.

The bell chimed again and she hurried to answer before it woke Glorie. Her hand trembled as she reached for the brass knob. Butterflies fluttered in her stomach as she pulled open the door. She blinked in surprise and held the door wider.

"Regina?"

The girl's wide mouth trembled. "Elizabeth?"

"Come in, Regina. I haven't seen you for a long time. Why didn't you come to graduation?"

Regina tugged the loose-fitting flowered blouse over her worn jeans. Her blonde hair needed washing and brushing and her blue eyes had dark circles under them. "Does— Vera Johnson live here?"

"She's my mother." Elizabeth closed the door just as a moth flew in to flutter around the hall light. She frowned up at it, then walked Regina to the family room. "Did you want to see Mom? She's away tonight with the family, but she'll be home about eleven."

"Are you . . . alone?" Regina looked around, her face suddenly pale. She pushed her tangled hair away from her eyes.

Elizabeth shrugged. "I'm alone. Do you want to tell me what's troubling you? I haven't seen you since you dropped out of school last winter. Are you still living at home? Do you have a job?" Elizabeth sank down on the couch and Regina perched on the edge of Chuck's chair. "Tell me what's been going on with you. You once were very close to April and May. Are you still?"

Regina bit her lip and locked her thin hands together. "I need to talk to Mrs. Johnson. I need to now!"

Elizabeth heard the rising hysteria and she frantically searched her mind for the right words. "Do you want to stay here until she gets home?"

"Yes! Yes, I must!"

"What will your mother say?"

"She won't care if I never go home!"

"Oh, Regina!"

Giant tears filled Regina's sad blue eyes and then burst out and she sobbed brokenly, her thin shoulders shaking. Elizabeth hesitated, then sat on the arm of the chair and wrapped her arms around Regina and pulled her close.

Why was it so urgent for Regina to see

Vera? Elizabeth frowned. She didn't even know that they knew each other. She and Regina had seen each other in school, but that was all. The Brakie twins were friends with her and talked often of her, but they hadn't in the last few months.

Finally the tears stopped and Regina shuddered and blew her nose and wiped her eyes with a tissue Elizabeth handed to her from the box on the end table.

"My life is ruined, Elizabeth!" wailed Regina, lifting red-rimmed eyes to Elizabeth.

Elizabeth gasped and plucked at the throw pillow beside her. "Do you want to tell me why you feel that way?"

Regina sniffed hard and rubbed her hand across her nose. She suddenly looked fourteen instead of eighteen. "I don't know where to start."

Silently Elizabeth prayed for the wisdom to help Regina. "Maybe you should tell me why it's so important for you to see Mom."

Before Regina could speak, Glorie's loud cry drifted downstairs and both Regina and Elizabeth jumped up.

"I thought you said you were alone," said Regina sharply.

"I am. I'm taking care of baby Glorie, but she's upstairs and, I thought, asleep for the night. I must go see about her. Will you come with me?"

Regina nodded, suddenly very tense, and Elizabeth looked questioningly at her, then led the way upstairs to the crib where Glorie lay kicking and screaming.

The dim light showed the fuzzy-headed baby, her face red and her mouth open wide and her light blanket kicked completely off. Before Elizabeth could make a move to pick up the baby, Regina gave a glad cry and scooped up the baby and held her close, crooning softly.

Elizabeth frowned and suddenly felt very helpless. "She probably needs her diaper changed." She reached for her but Regina jerked back, her mouth set in a stubborn line. "I want to change her," said Elizabeth as she once again reached for her.

Regina shook her head and held on tighter. "She's mine! You can't have her! You can't touch her!"

"Yours?" Elizabeth's eyes widened and she dropped her hands to her sides. "What are you talking about, Regina?"

"You knew I had a baby. Everyone in the entire school knew!"

"Yes, but. . . ."

"This is my baby. Glorie. She's mine!" Regina showered Glorie with kisses. "I was afraid I'd never find her!"

Glorie opened her mouth and cried loudly again and Regina picked up a diaper and carefully and lovingly changed her diaper and gown, then wrapped her in a soft pink blanket and held her to her heart.

Elizabeth sank to the edge of the queen-sized bed that Chuck and Vera shared. "I am surprised, Regina. How did you find out we had your baby? And why do we have her?"

Regina picked up the pacifier and pushed it into Glorie's mouth. She sucked loudly for a minute, then quietly. Regina sat in the rocker in the corner of the room with Glorie on her shoulder and gently rocked back and forth. "She feels so good! She smells so beautiful!"

"Vera takes very good care of her."

"I can see that." Regina smiled and mother and baby looked like a beautiful painting. "I used to give her a bath and dress her in little baby clothes that I bought at a garage sale last fall. Mom got mad at me because she said I was wasting my life on Glorie. She said I was too young to have a baby tie me down, but I love Glorie! I didn't want her when I first found out I was pregnant, but when I went to get an abortion and I saw pictures of what babies looked like inside their mothers, I couldn't do it. I couldn't kill my very own baby! I wanted her even if Doug wouldn't look at me again. He didn't care about the baby. He let me do what I wanted to do and he never talked to me again." Regina lifted her chin and her eyes flashed. "But I didn't care! I had a baby inside me and I wasn't going to kill her!"

Elizabeth looked at Glorie and a bitter taste filled her mouth as she thought about Regina having an abortion. It would have been terrible! "But I still don't know how we got Glorie."

"Ms. Kremeen!" Regina spit out the name and Elizabeth could only nod. "She came and took Glorie and then she wouldn't tell me where she'd placed her! I begged and begged, but she wouldn't tell."

"How did you find out?"

"I went to Social Services today and when she was out of her office I sneaked in and looked in the file. I didn't want to do that, but I had to! I had to find Glorie and get her back!"

Elizabeth's heart sank. Ms. Kremeen would fight like crazy to have her own way. She didn't want Glorie back with Regina, and she'd do everything in her power to keep them apart. "You can't just take Glorie or you'll be in trouble with the police, Regina."

"I don't care! I want my baby and I'm going to have her!"

"Oh, dear," Elizabeth said weakly.

"Mom called Ms. Kremeen and told her I wasn't a fit mother; then Ms. Kremeen came and looked at the dump we live in and she took Glorie away." Tears filled Regina's eyes and slowly slipped down her flushed cheeks. The baby whimpered, sucked the pacifier louder, then was quiet. Regina pressed her cheek against the soft head. "Mom said she wouldn't take care of Glorie while I was at work and I couldn't hire someone. I didn't have enough money to do that. And I won't raise Glorie on welfare! I won't!"

Elizabeth nodded. She knew how terrible it had been to be called "aid kid" all her life until the Johnsons adopted her. "I want to help you, Regina, but I can't let you take Glorie."

Regina's face darkened. "You can't stop me!"

Elizabeth jumped up and rubbed her arms in agitation. "Listen to me, Regina. You don't want to lose Glorie forever. And you don't want to make trouble for Mom. We'll all help you. Dad will know what to do. He knows a lot of people and he will find a way to help you."

"I won't leave Glorie here! I can't be without her again!" Regina rocked harder, clutching Glorie to her chest in desperation.

Elizabeth walked to the window and looked out at the yard light and the circle of gold light it made on the lawn. Finally she turned back. "You stay here with us, Regina. You can share my room."

"Oh, Elizabeth! Oh, no! I couldn't ask you to keep me!"

Elizabeth sat on the edge of the bed and leaned forward earnestly. "It's the only answer, Regina. Call your mother and tell her that you're staying over with a friend so that she won't worry about you, then stay here. Mom and Dad will find a way for you to keep Glorie. I know they will! Ms. Kremeen will just have to live with it." Elizabeth chuckled and finally Regina smiled.

"I'll stay, Elizabeth. But if I see that things aren't working out for us, then I'm taking Glorie and running. I'll leave the state. I'll do anything to keep my baby!"

Elizabeth rubbed her hand up and down her cheek and frowned thoughtfully. "I hope this doesn't get Mom in trouble with Social Services." She shook her head. "She would want to help you no matter what."

Regina sniffed back tears. "Why are you doing this? Why would they want to help me?"

"God loves you and Glorie, and we love you."

Regina ducked her head. "April and May talk like that, too. They told me how God changed their lives, but I didn't really listen. If God can help me and Glorie, then I want him to. No one else cares about us."

"He can and he will," said Elizabeth with a firm shake of her head. Her curls bobbed and a warmth spread through her. "He wants what is the very best for both of you. He does love you, Regina."

Finally she lifted her eyes. "Tell me why."

"He made you and he loved you from the very beginning. All he wants from you is your love given back to him."

Quietly Elizabeth talked to Regina about God's great gift, his only Son, to mankind, given so that all could have abundant life. She told of God's peace and strength that would be hers the minute she confessed Jesus as Lord and Savior, and that a new spirit would be given to her.

Regina nodded several times and asked questions occasionally. Then she said, "I do want Jesus as my Lord and Savior. I'want God's peace and love and life."

Tears pricked Elizabeth's eyes as she prayed with Regina there in the bedroom. The only sounds, besides her voice, were Glorie's gentle breathing and the ticking of the clock on the nightstand.

Much later Regina carefully laid Glorie in the crib, then turned and hugged Elizabeth. "I feel so different! I came here full of fear and anger and pain. Now I'm full of love and peace!"

"I know what you mean," said Elizabeth softly as she wiped away her own tears. "I think right now it would be good if I found a gown and robe for you so you can take a shower and go to bed. You look exhausted and Glorie wakes up very early in the morning."

"Shouldn't I wait up to talk to Mrs. Johnson?"

"No. I'll talk to my parents and then tomorrow we'll make plans for you and Glorie."

While Regina was in the shower, Elizabeth changed the sheets on her bed, then pulled back the covers. She looked around and bit her bottom lip. Just what would Chuck and Vera say about Regina being here?

Elizabeth laughed softly. This day had certainly turned out differently than she thought it would.

Regina was asleep when Elizabeth heard the family return. She ran downstairs, knowing they'd ask about the strange car in the drive.

"Mom, Dad, could we talk in the study?" she said quietly around the noise of the others.

Chuck scratched his red head and grinned. "What have you done this time, Elizabeth?"

"Whose car is outside?" asked Vera, looking quickly around.

"I'll tell you in the study."

Chuck and Vera said good night to the others and Vera added, "Please be very quiet upstairs. We don't want to wake the baby."

Elizabeth hid a smile. She wasn't the only

one they'd wake. She sat on a leather chair facing Chuck and Vera on the couch.

"You look ready to burst," said Chuck, studying her carefully.

Vera took Chuck's hand and gripped it. "I think I'm going to need a little support."

"Now, Mom, would I do anything to make you apprehensive?"

Vera laughed. "Yes. Now, tell us before I start to think the worst. You didn't bring in another runaway."

Elizabeth shook her head, knowing Vera was thinking of the time she'd hidden April and May from a caseworker and their foster family. She took a deep breath and told them about Regina Brook. "And she's asleep in my room right now."

"Oh, my," said Vera.

"I'm glad you had her stay," said Chuck. "We'll help her somehow. But first thing in the morning I will have to call Ms. Kremeen and tell her what's going on."

"Oh, my," said Vera again, her eyes wide. "She won't like this at all."

"Her job is to help people, not hurt them," said Chuck sharply. "I think it's time she learned that. I'll talk to Mr. Cinder to make sure no harm comes to us or the baby."

Elizabeth leaned back with a pleased smile. She crossed her legs and listened as Chuck talked. What a terrific family she had!

Eight
A change in Mrs. Briggs

"Joan, your mother's here again," whispered Elizabeth frantically to the woman in the bed.

Joan lifted herself up tiredly. "It doesn't matter, Elizabeth. I told her the truth last night. She came again when David was here and we realized that we were wrong in trying to keep your good work a secret. We told her that you and Jerry and some of the church ladies have helped us."

"Was she angry?"

Joan sighed. "Yes, but she'll get over it."

"Jerry's letting her in, so I'll go back to work and leave you two alone." Elizabeth gripped the dustcloth tighter. What would she do if Mrs. Briggs asked her to leave? "You call me if you want anything."

"I do want to sit on the couch for a while. Could you help me with my robe?"

Elizabeth picked up the worn, flowered robe and Joan wearily pushed her arms into the sleeves.

"I don't want to scare you, Elizabeth," said Joan softly. "But I think I'll be going to the hospital today."

Elizabeth gasped in alarm and shivers ran over her body. "What shall I do? Should I call David?"

"Not until I know for sure." Joan groaned and leaned heavily against Elizabeth just as Mrs. Briggs walked in.

"Why are you out of bed?" asked Mrs. Briggs, taking Joan's arm. "I came to take care of you and here you are walking around."

Joan looked at her mother with her brows raised questioningly.

Mrs. Briggs flushed. "I can't very well let others take care of my own daughter and grandchildren and not lift a finger, can I?"

Elizabeth saw the sparkle of tears in Mrs. Briggs' eyes and she smiled. "Joan wants to sit up for a while. Shall we both help her to the couch?"

Mrs. Briggs hesitated, then nodded. "You and that boy outdoors playing with the children have been a big help and I want to thank you. It was hard for me to get used to the idea of my family out in the country and away from me, but I have to admit they are happy and they do have good friends."

Joan sank down on the couch and pushed trembling fingers through her hair. "Mom, I'm glad you're here. And I know Elizabeth is, too."

"She thinks it's time to have the baby," said Elizabeth quickly. "I don't know what to do."

Mrs. Briggs squared her shoulders and lifted her rounded chin. "I do. I'm just glad I didn't miss this day because of my stubbornness."

"Now, Mother, no more of that. I didn't want to admit that I still need you very much, but I do need you and you need me. What's past is past."

Mrs. Briggs nodded and smiled stiffly. "We'll leave it at that." She turned to Elizabeth. "You call David. Then, if you can, will you stay with the children until I get back later? I intend to stay here while Joan's in the hospital."

"Mother! Oh, thank you!"

"It's the least I can do!"

"Are you sure you want to, Mom?"

"Joan, I am going to take care of my grandchildren and get to know them. It's past time for me to be a real grandmother. And soon I'll have a new grandchild." She smiled. "A new grandchild. Well, I can't just stand around. Let's get you packed and to the hospital."

"I have time, Mom."

"It takes more than half an hour to get to town and I won't have you making it just in time to deliver!" Mrs. Briggs tugged on Joan's arm and finally Joan stood up, her face pale. Mrs. Briggs turned to Elizabeth. "What are you waiting for? Call David and tell him to meet us at the hospital. And tell him to bring flowers. I don't want him to forget that."

Elizabeth walked to the kitchen to the phone, shaking her head. Mrs. Briggs certainly knew how to give orders and take over. But her loud bark covered up a soft heart.

Elizabeth dialed the number and waited a long time before David finally reached the phone. She gave him the messages, then listened as he talked excitedly. "She really is all right, David. Her mother is driving her to the hospital. Honestly, you don't have to worry about a thing. No, Mrs. Briggs isn't upsetting Joan. She's helping her. You'll see when you meet her at the hospital."

Finally he calmed down enough to hang up and Elizabeth shook her head and clicked her tongue.

Just then she heard Scottie shouting

playfully to the twins and she turned from the phone to look out the window. Did Jerry guess that she'd once again brought Scottie to keep from being alone with him even for a minute? He hadn't seemed to notice. He'd smiled into her eyes, but he hadn't said anything that would make her more nervous about being alone with him. Maybe he had given up on her.

An icy band tightened around her heart and she stood at the window and watched him play with the kids in the yard. The warm wind blew his unruly brown hair and sweat stained his shirt. He was laughing and running and totally enjoying playing with Scottie and the Vincents.

She turned away, suddenly feeling very left out. She'd planned to help Joan today, but Mrs. Briggs had taken over. Jerry was taking charge of the kids and she wasn't really needed at all.

She really could've stayed home with Regina today, but even Regina didn't need her since Vera and Chuck were taking charge of everything.

Elizabeth rubbed her hands down her jeans and looked around the already clean kitchen. Who did need her? Just then Adam's face came before her and she nodded. Adam needed her badly. Hadn't he said so often enough?

She smiled and suddenly felt better.

Mrs. Briggs walked in smelling of a strong perfume. "Elizabeth, I want to apologize for being so rude to you yesterday," she said stiffly, almost coldly. "I was wrong."

"That's all right. I'm glad that you're here now when Joan needs you."

"I'll call the doctor's office and tell him that we're coming in. I'll try not to be very late. I'm sure you and Jerry have things you want to do. Joan tells me that you're a concert pianist."

Elizabeth nodded.

"I'd like to hear you play. I have a fine piano at my house." She sighed. "I have a large house and no one to share it with." She shrugged her plump shoulders, then picked up the phone and dialed.

Elizabeth listened to her sharp, decisive instructions. Mrs. Briggs hung up and nodded in satisfaction.

"Now then, I know they'll take good care of Joan. I won't have her just another maternity patient!" She tugged her flowered dress down and marched out of the small kitchen.

Elizabeth hurried after her and carefully helped Joan out the door to the waiting car. The kids ran to them and pressed against them. Joan kissed them good-bye, even

Scottie; then they all stood together, waving as Mrs. Briggs drove out in a cloud of dust.

A robin sang in a tree branch. The dog lay at Elizabeth's feet, panting loudly. Neddie gripped Elizabeth's legs and begged to be picked up. She lifted him to her hip and held him.

Jerry caught her eye and smiled and winked and she quickly ducked her head.

"I thought Grandma hated us," said Diane.

"She doesn't," said Shane.

"I've got a grandma," said Scottie and he proceeded to tell them about Grandma and Grandpa Johnson and they listened to every word.

"I wanna eat," said Neddie. "Did you bring candy?"

Jerry laughed and Elizabeth kissed Neddie's dirty cheek.

Three hours later Mrs. Briggs drove back in and Elizabeth rushed with the others to meet her as she slid out of the car. She carried a bag of groceries and Jerry took them and she looked at him in surprise, then smiled.

"Did she have a baby yet?" asked Scottie.

"Not yet," said Mrs. Briggs, looking down at Scottie as if she'd just seen the kids standing around her. She looked at the others without a smile. "Follow Jerry to the kitchen and he'll give you a special treat that I brought for you."

"Is it candy?" asked Neddie without a smile.

Mrs. Briggs studied him, then finally said, "Yes."

Neddie blinked, then laughed and flung himself at her legs and she stumbled back against the car. "Thank you! Candy! Candy!"

She pried him loose and he ran after Jerry and she shook her head. "My, he does like candy."

Elizabeth nodded. "How is Joan, Mrs. Briggs?"

She moistened her red lips with the tip of her tongue. "Not very well, but I didn't want to alarm the children. The doctor is very worried."

"Oh, no!"

"She said not to worry because God was with her."

Elizabeth saw the question and the hope in Mrs. Briggs' eyes. "God is with her. He will give her strength and help right now when she needs it. We'll ask him to help her deliver a fine healthy baby."

Mrs. Briggs sniffed and dabbed her eyes. "Yes, well, you do that if you would."

"We will and my family will be praying also. God does answer, Mrs. Briggs."

"Joan seemed to think he would." She

walked stiffly to the door, then stopped. "You and Jerry can go home now. I will call you when I hear anything."

"Thank you." Suddenly Elizabeth slipped her arms around Mrs. Briggs and hugged her, then kissed her rosy cheek. "Joan'll be all right. You'll see."

Mrs. Briggs pulled away, clearing her throat. "I hope so."

Elizabeth turned to go, then turned back. "Mrs. Briggs, have you ever thought about sharing your home with homeless people?"

Mrs. Briggs' eyes widened. "Oh, my, no! I have Joan!"

"But she has a family and she said that you have a large house, that you get lonely."

Mrs. Briggs twisted her hands in agitation. "I don't know why Joan would talk of this to you."

"She didn't do it to embarrass you. She loves you. She doesn't want you to be lonely and I think I know of a way so that you won't be."

"And how is that?" she asked stiffly.

Elizabeth hesitated, suddenly apprehensive about what she was doing. But she'd gone this far. It was too late to back out now. Almost in one breath she told her about Regina and baby Glorie. "They need a home and love and help, Mrs. Briggs."

"Yes, well, I can understand that, but I'm

afraid it isn't my kind of thing to do. But I will give it some thought. You run along now."

Elizabeth smiled, then walked to the kitchen to find Jerry and Scottie.

Nine
Advice from Adam

"Jerry, if Adam is home, drop me off there, please." Elizabeth saw Jerry's jaw tighten and her stomach fluttered. She saw his quick glance in the back seat at Scottie and she knew if Scottie hadn't been there, Jerry would've had a lot to say. Her ears burned just thinking about it.

"It's going to be strange not going to help the Vincents," said Jerry finally. "I do think I'll go once in a while and help with the garden and lawn."

Scottie jumped forward. "May I go with you to play with the twins? They said they'd come play with me and their grandma said she might bring them over."

"Did she?" Elizabeth raised her brows in surprise. "Mrs. Briggs is really trying to be helpful to Joan and the grandchildren, isn't she?"

Jerry nodded. "The kids and I were praying for her. God knew the family needed a miracle."

Elizabeth peeked out of the corner of her eye at Jerry and she wanted to tell him that he was wonderful, but she sat very still with her hands folded primly in her lap.

Jerry braked and pulled the car into Adam's drive. A dog barked. A crow cawed from a pine bough. "I'll talk to you later, Elizabeth," Jerry said, his eyes dark with an emotion that Elizabeth couldn't—or wouldn't—read. "Call me when you hear something about Joan, will you?"

"Of course." She slipped out of the car into the hot sunlight, then leaned down to see Scottie. "Tell the family that I'll be home soon."

He nodded, then leaned up to talk to Jerry just as Jerry spun gravel as he backed out. Elizabeth stood hesitantly in the drive, then walked briskly toward the house. She had to talk to Adam.

Just as she reached the porch, the door opened and Adam walked out with a happy greeting. Lapdog rushed out, barking and wriggling around Elizabeth's feet. Adam shushed Lapdog with a stern command, then said, "This is a pleasant surprise, Elizabeth. Can you sit awhile?" He motioned toward the porch swing. He was dressed in new jeans and a short-sleeved knit shirt. His curly brown hair looked freshly brushed.

"I'd rather take a walk, if that's all right with you. I don't think I can sit still right now."

"What has happened to make you so tense?" He fell into step beside her and they walked toward the woods.

She tugged at the collar on her sleeveless blouse. "It's a lot of things, Adam."

"Tell me, Elizabeth."

She felt like bursting into tears, but she forced a bright smile. "I guess my life just isn't turning out like I'd planned."

He held a branch aside and she walked ahead of him along the trail. "I know helping the Vincents has taken a lot of your time that you would've spent in practicing."

Elizabeth stopped and turned to face Adam. "Joan went to the hospital and Mrs. Briggs said it doesn't look good. She just has to be all right! It would be terrible if anything happened to her!"

"Hey, don't get so upset!" He caught her icy hand and held it firmly. "I know you probably prayed for her. God is on the job helping Joan. You don't have to carry the worry of it."

Elizabeth sniffed hard and nodded. "I

know," she said in a tiny voice. "It's just that it's so important to me and to her family and to Mrs. Briggs."

"God loves Joan and her family, Elizabeth. He'll take care of her."

"I know. Also I told Mrs. Briggs about Regina and baby Glorie and asked her if she would take them in and now I think that was a big mistake."

"Why? I think it sounds great."

"But Mrs. Briggs has never done that kind of thing and I guess I should have kept my mouth shut. I don't know why I even suggested it."

"But you did and you can't take it back, so forget it."

A mosquito landed on Elizabeth's arm and she swatted it before it could sting her. Small ground squirrels and chipmunks scurried through the underbrush. With a sigh Elizabeth shook her head. "You're right, Adam. I can't worry about anything with my concert coming up next week."

"I'm sure you're ready for it."

"Yes."

Slowly they walked deeper into the woods; then once again she stopped and turned back, her face white. "Jerry is jealous of you, Adam. He said he doesn't want me to see you again."

Adam shook his head in bewilderment.

"What has gotten into Jerry? I thought we were friends."

"I know. But he has this crazy notion that he loves me and he thinks that I'm falling in love with you and he doesn't want me to see you again. He even suggested that I am in love with him! Isn't that ridiculous?"

Adam crossed his arms and studied Elizabeth thoughtfully. "I have thought at times that you're in love with Jerry."

"What? You, too? Oh, dear."

"Calm down. What's so bad about being in love with Jerry? He's a great guy."

"But it doesn't fit in with my future plans! What about my piano? He wants more of my time!"

"Elizabeth, you know that you must take time for others. Don't block out love just because it doesn't fit in with your plans. You can still be a concert pianist even if you love Jerry. You know you can."

Later they walked back to the yard and Elizabeth wiped perspiration from her face, then accepted the cup of cold well water that Adam held out to her.

She drank and the cold water slipped down her parched throat and relieved the dryness. She handed back the cup and wiped the back of her hand across her mouth.

"We are still good friends, aren't we, Elizabeth?"

She saw the concern on his face and she squeezed his hand and smiled. "We will always be good friends, Adam. Always!"

"I'm glad. You're very important to me."

"And you to me." She laughed softly. "I'll think about what you said. I promise."

He hugged her with a grin; then let her go. "Are you too tired to walk home? I'll drive you."

She shook her head. "Thanks, anyway. I'll walk and enjoy it."

Several minutes later she walked into her house and smelled the supper cooking and her stomach grumbled with hunger. She heard the baby crying and she hurried to the family room and peeked in to find Regina and Glorie with Vera.

"Hi," said Elizabeth. "How'd it go today?"

Vera laughed and Regina grinned and hugged Glorie tighter.

Elizabeth sat on Chuck's chair and leaned back and crossed her long legs. It felt wonderful to sit down. "I want to hear what Ms. Kremeen said and did."

Vera leaned forward and dropped her needlework in the basket beside her chair. "Ms. Kremeen came flying out here the minute she had free time this afternoon and she demanded that I give Glorie up or send Regina packing. Since we already had word from Mr. Cinder that we could keep the baby and that he'd give Regina visiting rights,

Ms. Kremeen couldn't insist on anything. She left in a huff but she said she'd be back with the authority to take Glorie away from us and keep her away from Regina for good."

Regina shivered. "It scared me, but Vera said that God will take care of us."

"And he will!" Vera said with a firm nod.

"I think we need to find a home for both of you," said Elizabeth with a smile at Regina. "That would settle everything."

"Dad's working on it," said Vera. "He said he'd make a couple of calls today, then let us know. Something will open up."

Elizabeth rubbed her hand down her jeans. "Did Scottie tell you that Joan went to the hospital?"

Vera nodded. "I hope she has an easy time."

Elizabeth thought about what Mrs. Briggs had said and she said fervently, "Me, too!"

Just then the phone rang and Elizabeth jumped, then rushed to Vera's little desk and answered. She sank to the chair when she heard Mrs. Briggs' voice. "Have you heard anything yet?"

"She had a girl."

Elizabeth smiled. "A girl! That makes the family perfect, doesn't it? Two boys and two girls. And how is Joan?"

"Just fine. The doctor said it was amazing. David will be home soon so I must fix supper, but if it's all right with you I'll bring the children over tomorrow morning to play with Scottie."

"That's perfect, Mrs. Briggs. I know he'll love it. If you need any help, let me know."

Mrs. Briggs was quiet a long time, then said, "I'll get along just fine. Diane is a big help and so is Shane. And Neddie, too."

Elizabeth chuckled. She knew the kids had probably been listening and Mrs. Briggs had said their names to make them feel good. "Thanks for calling. I'm glad to know that Joan and the baby are well. We'll see you in the morning."

"About ten."

"Good-bye."

"Wait." Mrs. Briggs was silent for several seconds and Elizabeth wondered if she'd heard correctly. "Have the girl and her child found a home?"

"No."

"All right. I was only curious." She said good-bye softly and the dial tone buzzed in Elizabeth's ear.

She hung up and turned with a smile and told her news of Joan and the baby. "I must tell Jerry." She picked up the phone, then replaced it with a clatter. "I'll call from the study."

She rushed out before Vera or Regina could see her flushed face. Scottie called to her from the kitchen door and she stopped and told him the news. He grinned, then whooped with excitement when she told him that Mrs. Briggs was bringing the children to play tomorrow. He ran off to share the news with Toby, and Elizabeth walked into the study and closed the door. She leaned against it and looked at the phone on Chuck's large oak desk. She bit her lip, then locked the study door and walked to the desk.

She dialed and at the sound of Jerry's voice, she dropped down into Chuck's chair, the receiver clutched tightly in her damp hand.

"Mrs. Briggs just called to let us know Joan had a girl and they're both doing well."

"I'm glad."

"Mrs. Briggs is bringing the kids over to play with Scottie in the morning."

"That's nice. He'll have fun."

She twisted the white cord and tried to think of something more to say. For some strange reason she didn't want to hang up.

"How was your visit with Adam?" Jerry asked stiffly.

She hesitated, swallowed hard, then said, "Just fine." Why couldn't she say good-bye and hang up? "Is it time for you to go to work?"

"I'm not working tonight."

"Oh. You're not sick, are you?"

"Would you care?"

"Oh, Jerry!"

"Would you?"

She gripped the receiver tighter and stared at the path the sun made across the carpet. "Of course I would care. I don't want you to be sick, Jerry."

"I love you, Elizabeth."

She froze, then dropped the receiver in place with a bang. Her heart raced and she pressed her hands to her fiery cheeks.

The phone rang and she jumped, then reached to answer it, then pulled back. It was probably Jerry. Should she answer it? It rang again, then was quiet. She waited. Perspiration dotted her forehead. No one called to say it was for her.

She sat with her head lifted to catch any sound, then sagged in relief when she finally realized that the call hadn't been for her.

She picked up a yellow pencil and studied it with great care, then laid it down again next to the stapler.

Abruptly she pushed herself up and walked to the door. Impatiently she unlocked the door and rushed out, out to be with others so that she wouldn't have to think about Jerry or hear his words over and over in her mind.

Ten
Happy endings

Elizabeth smiled as Mrs. Briggs sat beside
her at the picnic table. The kids played noisily
in the yard and Snowball nickered over the
fence in the pen near the horse barn.

"Joan and the baby are getting stronger
every day," said Mrs. Briggs with an
unusually bright smile. "They've been home
for two weeks now and we're all enjoying
little Lorna."

"I think that it was sweet of Joan and
David to name the baby after you."

Mrs. Briggs looked as humble as she
could. "It did please me a great deal." She
shooed a fly away from her arm. "Your
concert the other night was wonderful.
Thank you for the ticket."

111

"I'm glad I could share it with you."

"I sat just behind your friend Jerry. It was nice to see him again."

Elizabeth's heart stood still. She hadn't realized Jerry had gone to the concert. He hadn't spoken to her since she'd slammed the receiver down in his ear. And she didn't deserve to have him speak to her, or love her.

The back door opened and Regina walked out with Glorie in her arms. Regina looked clean and healthy and not at all the worn, tattered girl that she'd been when she first walked into the Johnsons' house.

"Hello, Mrs. Briggs." Regina sat down and smiled happily. "It's good to see you again."

Mrs. Briggs nodded. "I had a talk with Mr. Cinder yesterday," she said stiffly and Elizabeth looked at her in surprise. "I told him that I'd like to have you and the baby move in with me. He said that if you did he would insist that Ms. Kremeen give up the idea of keeping you and your baby apart."

Regina gulped, her eyes wide in surprise.

Mrs. Briggs brushed a speck of dust off her sleeve. "I have plenty of room in my house for you and the baby. If it would please you, then I would like to have you live with me for as long as you want."

"That is very nice of you," said Elizabeth, smiling with pleasure.

"It is," said Regina. "But I don't think

112

you know what it would be like having a baby around."

"But, my dear, I do! My daughter just had a baby and I know what to expect." She cleared her throat and looked around, then back at Regina. "My house is very empty and I get lonely. It would please me very much to have you and Glorie live with me."

"Oh, Mrs. Briggs!" Regina blinked back tears. "I don't know what to say."

"I would be willing to watch Glorie while you work. She's a very precious baby and I know I won't have any trouble with her."

Regina squeezed Mrs. Briggs' hand. "I would like to live with you. You are a dear friend. Thank you."

Mrs. Briggs flushed and said, "Yes, well, you can move in when you are ready."

"Today would be fine with me," said Regina. "Elizabeth, I know you'll be glad for privacy in your room again. I will never forget what you and your family have done for me."

"We were glad to help." Elizabeth smiled. Her eyes swam with tears at the happiness she saw on Regina's face.

"I'll go tell Vera the plan," said Regina as she stood up.

"I'll go with you," said Mrs. Briggs. "Let me carry Glorie. Your arms must be tired." She carefully took Glorie and held her close to her chest and smiled down at her. Glorie cooed and smiled back. Mrs. Briggs looked back at Elizabeth. "Thank you for the suggestion."

Just as the door closed behind them Scottie ran to Elizabeth. His face was damp with sweat and his hair wind-blown. "Is Jerry coming today, Elizabeth?"

"I don't know." Her pulse leaped at the thought of seeing Jerry. "Did he say he would?"

"I'm going home tomorrow and he said he'd come say good-bye." Scottie looked toward the road with a scowl. "Will you call him and ask if he will come today?"

She swallowed hard. "You can call him, Scottie."

"But I have company right now. If we wait too long, then he'll go to work and won't come see me." Scottie turned his wide blue eyes on Elizabeth. "Please. Please, you call him. Please!"

She sighed and nodded. "All right. I will."

"Right now?"

She glanced at her watch. "Yes."

"Good! Go call right now!"

She nodded.

He nudged her. "Right now, Elizabeth."

She laughed and stood up. "Run and play, Scottie. I'll come back out and tell you what he said."

She walked slowly into the house. Soft music drifted from the study and the smell

114

of coffee filled the hall. Oh, but she didn't want to call Jerry. What if he hung up on her? What if he refused to talk to her? It would certainly serve her right!

She peeked into the study, then walked in and closed and locked the door. Her legs trembled as she walked to the phone. Two weeks ago she'd called Jerry, then hung up on him. He hadn't called back or tried to see her or talk to her in church.

She flipped back her curls. Well, she was glad that he'd finally gotten the message.

Reluctantly she dialed his number and when he answered she sagged against the desk, her mouth suddenly dry, her body limp.

"Hi, it's me—Elizabeth."

There was silence and she panicked and almost dropped the phone. "Jerry?"

"What?"

"I told Scottie that I'd call."

"Oh. Scottie. I should've known." He sounded bitter and she felt her throat tighten.

"He's going home tomorrow and he wants you to come see him before he goes. Could you come now?" She waited tensely, barely breathing.

"I'll be there in fifteen minutes. Does that give you enough time to run away from me?"

She gasped. "What do you mean?"

"Never mind." He hung up and the dial tone buzzed loudly in her ear and finally she dropped the receiver in place, then just stood at the desk with her head down, her shoulders drooping.

What had she done to Jerry?

She shook her head until her curls bounced, then lifted her pointed chin high. She hadn't done a thing to him! And she certainly wouldn't give him the privilege of seeing her run away! She would walk right up to him and speak to him just as she had all these years.

She forced a smile as she squared her shoulders and walked out of the study. She glanced down at her jeans and suddenly wished that she had on something really gorgeous so that he'd notice. What was she thinking? She didn't need to look gorgeous for Jerry. Besides, she couldn't look gorgeous if she tried. She wasn't Susan.

A few minutes later Elizabeth stood near the garage, her hands locked behind her back, her heart racing faster than Snowball ran. Scottie jumped up and down, shouting excitedly.

Jerry slowly drove in and stood beside his car and looked over Scottie's head at Elizabeth. She nodded and he did; then he turned his attention to Scottie.

"So, Scottie, tomorrow's the big day. I'm going to miss you."

"I gotta go home and take care of

116

Mom and my new baby brother. I can't wait until he gets bigger so I can play ball with him."

They walked off together and Elizabeth stood in the drive and watched them and her heart rose in her throat and almost choked her. Jerry looked back at her and she saw the white scar on his face as he turned. She clenched and unclenched her fists and her chest rose and fell. She wanted to call to him and run after him and hold out her arms to him. She wanted to hear him say again that he loved her. She wanted to tell him that she loved him.

She clamped her hand over her mouth and stared wide-eyed at Jerry's back.

She loved him!

But that was impossible! This was Jerry Grosbeck, the boy she'd known and loved as a brother for years. She couldn't *love* him! But she did. Somehow her feelings had changed and she had yearned to run to him and tell him, but she walked listlessly across the yard to the swing. With a heavy sigh she sat in the swing and gently pushed herself back and forth.

She looked at her hands gripping the rope and she knew she should go in and practice her piano, but she couldn't move. What was wrong with her?

Snowball nickered for her but she couldn't go to her and pet her and talk to

her. A car drove past, then a noisy pickup.
Would she spend the rest of the morning
glued to the swing? She wrinkled her nose
and shook her head. As soon as Jerry drove
out, she'd walk into the house and help
Regina and Glorie get ready to leave; then
she'd practice the piano.

Why hadn't she seen Jerry at the concert?
She'd looked so carefully for him, but she
couldn't find him and it had been hard to
get into her music.

Jerry's car started and Elizabeth jerked to a
stop and watched as he slowly backed the
car down the long drive. Her mouth felt dry
and her tongue seemed glued to the roof of
her mouth. Why couldn't she run to him
and tell him that she wanted to talk to
him?

She saw him look at her and she lifted her
hand and motioned for him to come to her;
then her hand dropped down to her lap. Her
heart almost jumped out of her tee shirt.

He hesitated, then stopped and turned off
the ignition. She waited, then slowly stood
up and walked toward him. Still he didn't
move. She stopped and her eyes locked with
his. Panic seized her and she would've fled,
but she couldn't move.

Slowly he slid out of the car and walked
the few remaining steps to her. "Did you
want me?" His voice was husky and she saw
a muscle jump in his jaw. The white scar

seemed to stand out boldly on his sun-browned face and he absently fingered it. "Did you want me?" he said again, this time barely above a whisper.

"Yes," she said hoarsely.

His eyes seemed to devour her and she wanted to step into his arms, but fear of his rejection held her back. "Anything special?" he asked.

"Yes."

"What?"

She licked her dry lips. "Scottie is going to miss you."

"I'll miss him."

"Mrs. Briggs invited Regina and Glorie to move in with her. They're going today."

"Good. They'll be good for each other." She saw the pinched look around his mouth and the dark rings around his eyes.

"I hear you went to my concert."

"Yes."

"I'm glad."

"You played beautifully, the best I've ever heard you play."

She smiled slightly. "Thank you."

He looked off across the yard. "I have to go."

"Do you?" Oh, he mustn't go yet!

"I have to work."

"But not until later." Could he hear the panic in her voice?

He nodded. "Not until later."

119

"Can we walk? Maybe talk awhile?"

His jaw tightened. "What is there to say, Elizabeth? I've said it all and you pretend not to listen or care." He turned and she caught his arm and he looked down at her hand, then into her face. "Did you stop me so that you could tell me about your wedding plans with Adam?"

She dropped her hand to her side. "No!"

"No wedding?"

"No wedding."

"Good." He turned to go again and she bit her lip to keep from crying out.

Just as he reached for the car door she said, "Wait!"

He rubbed his forehead and groaned, then lifted an anguished face to her. "Wait for what, Elizabeth?"

She took a deep breath and let it out in a rush. "I love you."

He shook his head. "Don't play games with me!"

"I love you." She took a step toward him and he scowled so hard she stopped.

"I can't take this, Elizabeth. You're playing with me and I hate it. Do you hear me? I don't want you to say you love me if you're only saying it to soothe me."

Her eyes shone with love for him. "Jerry Grosbeck, I do love you!"

He stared at her incredulously, then put his arms around her. Finally he lifted his

120

head. "It took you long enough to admit it," he said hoarsely.

She grinned. "I'm sorry. I guess I'm just a little blind in some areas."

He kissed her eyelids. "You're not blind now. I love you, Elizabeth."

Gently she touched the scar on his face and he turned his lips into her palm. "I love you, Jerry," she whispered softly. "I love you very much."